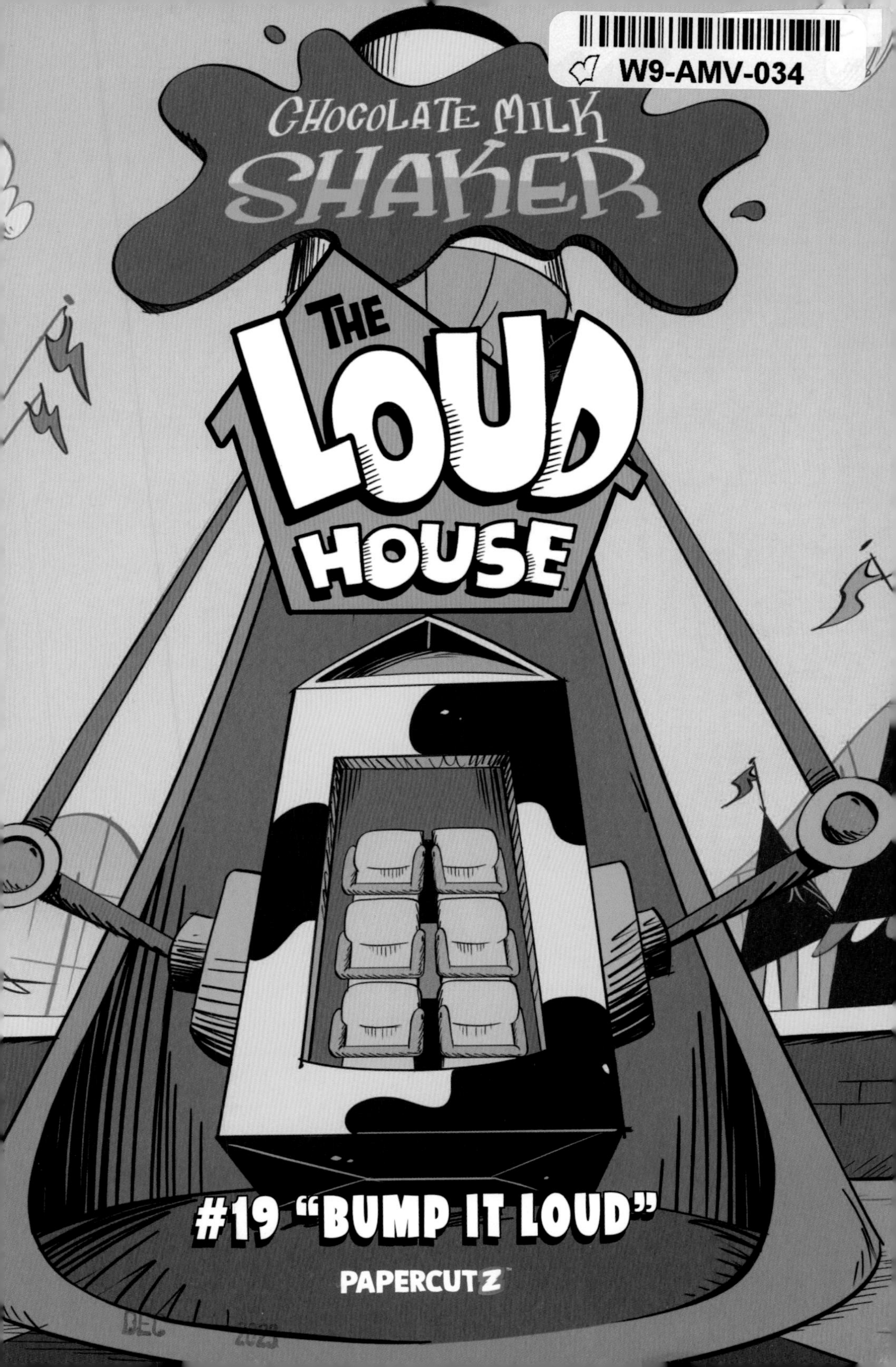

CHOCOLATE MILK
SHAKER
THE
LOUD
HOUSE
#19 "BUMP IT LOUD"
PAPERCUTZ

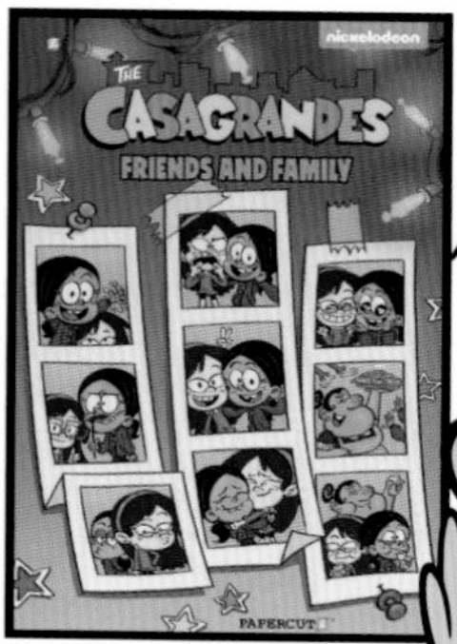
nickelodeon
THE CASAGRANDES
FRIENDS AND FAMILY
PAPERCUTZ

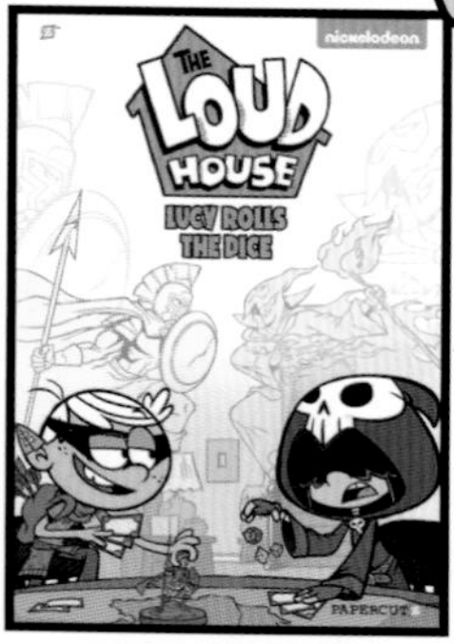
nickelodeon
THE LOUD HOUSE
LUCY ROLLS THE DICE
PAPERCUTZ

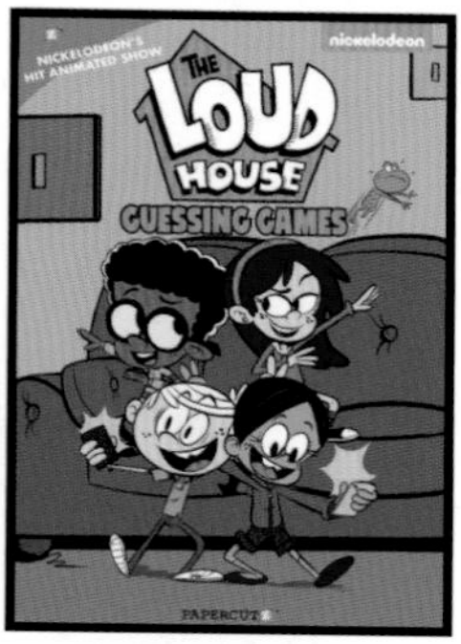
NICKELODEON'S HIT ANIMATED SHOW
nickelodeon
THE LOUD HOUSE
GUESSING GAMES
PAPERCUTZ

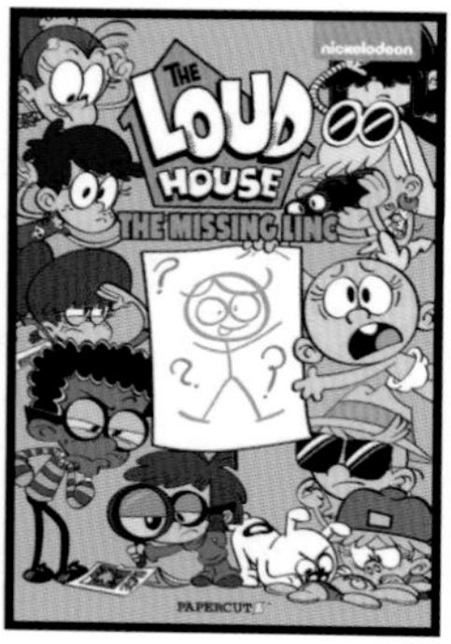
nickelodeon
THE LOUD HOUSE
THE MISSING LINC
PAPERCUTZ

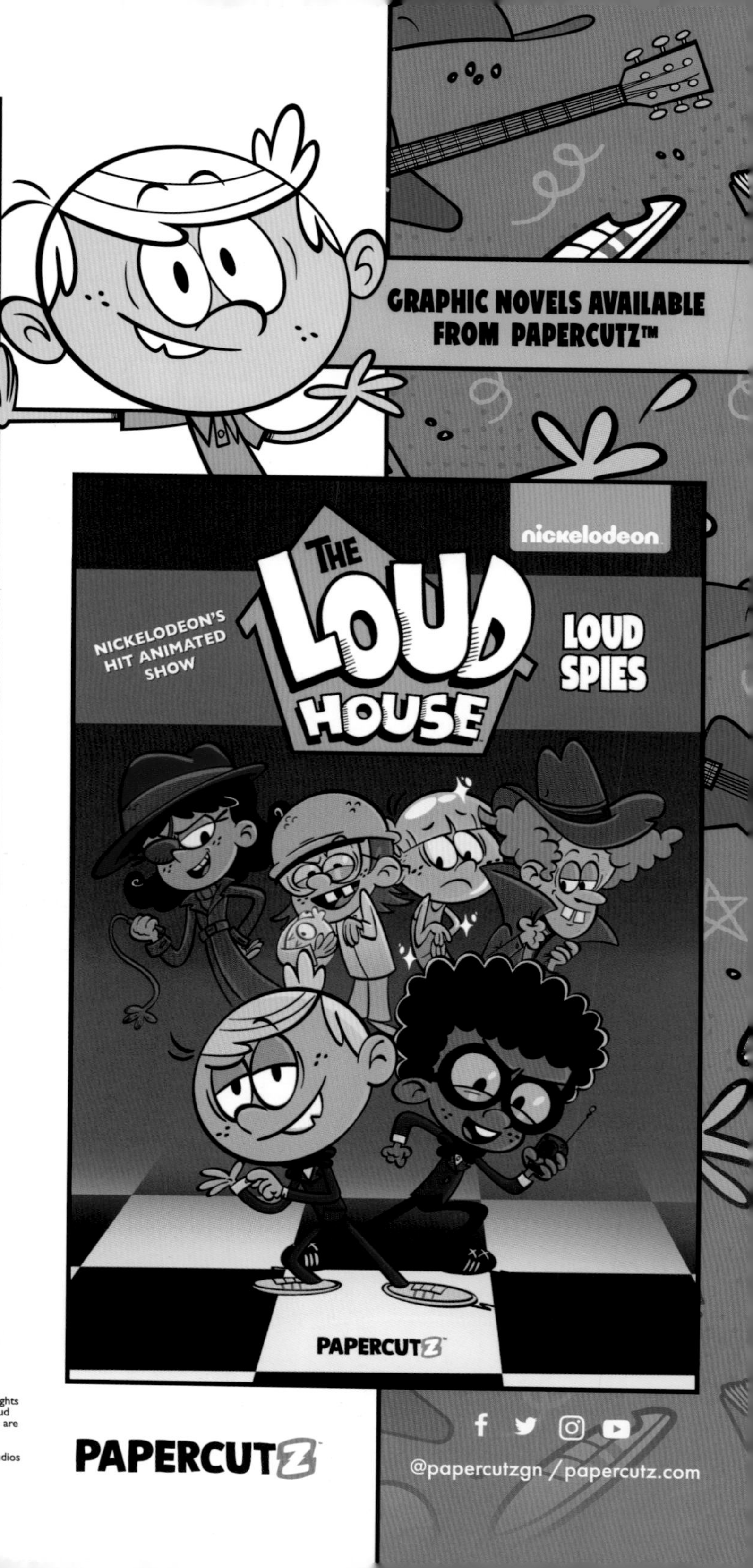
GRAPHIC NOVELS AVAILABLE
FROM PAPERCUTZ™
nickelodeon
NICKELODEON'S HIT ANIMATED SHOW
THE LOUD HOUSE
LOUD SPIES
PAPERCUTZ
@papercutzgn / papercutz.com

PAPERCUTZ

THE LOUD HOUSE

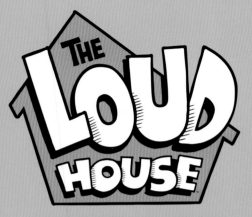

#19 "BUMP IT LOUD"

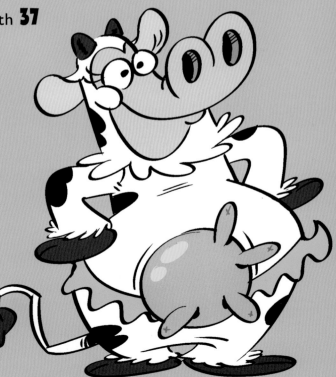

"TALL ENOUGH"
Mikey Levitt — Writer
Amanda Lioi — Artist, Colorist
Wilson Ramos Jr. — Letterer

"NOTHING BUT THE TOOTH"
Derek Fridolfs — Writer
Olivia Walden — Artist, Colorist
Bryan Senka — Letterer

"DON'T BE A DRAG"
Kiernan Sjursen-Lien — Writer
Lex Hobson — Artist, Colorist
Wilson Ramos Jr. — Letterer

"ONE MAN CROW"
Amanda Fein — Writer
Izzy Boyce-Blanchard — Artist, Colorist
Wilson Ramos Jr. — Letterer

"GAME SHAME"
Erik Steinman — Writer
Zazo Aguiar — Artist, Colorist
Wilson Ramos Jr. — Letterer

"MOO-MENTO"
Erik Steinman — Writer
Amanda Tran — Artist, Colorist
Wilson Ramos Jr. — Letterer

"TWO LOUDS A CROWD"
Amanda Lioi — Writer, Artist, Colorist
Wilson Ramos Jr. — Letterer

"BARN OF HORRORS"
Kevin Cannarile — Writer
Olivia Walden — Artist, Colorist
Wilson Ramos Jr. — Letterer

"PERFECT CHEESE"
Paloma Uribe — Writer
Melissa Kleynowski — Artist
Jose Hernandez — Colorist
Wilson Ramos Jr. — Letterer

"LUCKY STREAK"
Kayla Parker — Writer
Kelsey Wooley — Artist, Colorist
Wilson Ramos Jr. — Letterer

"THE NIGHT WALKER"
Mikey Levitt — Writer
Ryan Jampole — Artist
Erin Rodriguez — Colorist
Wilson Ramos Jr. — Letterer

LOUD HOUSE SPY SPECIAL PREVIEW
Erik Steinman — Writer
Lex Hobson — Artist, Colorist
Wilson Ramos Jr. — Letterer

LEX HOBSON — Cover Artist

JAYJAY JACKSON — Design

NEIL WADE, GABRIELLE DOLBEY, DANA CLUVERIUS, MOLLIE FREILICH, and ARTHUR "DJ" DESIN — Special Thanks

STEPHANIE BROOKS — Editor

JEFF WHITMAN — Comics Editor/Nickelodeon

MICOL HIATT — Comics Designer/Nickelodeon

MIKE MARTS — Editor in Chief

LAURA CHACÓN - Founder • MARK LONDON - CEO and Chief Creative Officer • MARK IRWIN - Senior Vice President • MIKE MARTS - EVP and Editor-in-Chief
CHRIS FERNANDEZ - Publisher • ZOHRA ASHPARI - Senior Editor • STEPHANIE BROOKS - Editor • GIOVANNA T. OROZCO - Production Manager
MIGUEL A. ZAPATA - Design Director • DIANA BERMÚDEZ - Graphic Designer • DAVID REYES - Graphic Designer • SEBASTIAN RAMIREZ - Graphic Designer
ADRIANA T. OROZCO - Interactive Media Designer • NICOLÁS ZEA ARIAS - Audiovisual Production • CECILIA MEDINA - Chief Financial Officer
STARLIN GONZALEZ - Accounting Director • KURT NELSON - Director of Sales • ALLISON POND - Marketing Director • MAYA LOPEZ - Marketing Manager
JAMES FACCINTO - Publicist • GEOFFREY LAPID - Sales & Marketing Specialist • SPENSER NELLIS - Marketing Coordinator
CHRIS LA TORRE - Retail Relations Manager • CHRISTINA HARRINGTON - Direct Market Sales Coordinator • PEDRO HERRERA - Retail Associate
FRANK SILVA - Executive Assistant • STEPHANIE HIDALGO - Office Manager

Papercutz was founded by Terry Nantier and Jim Salicrup.

ISBN: 978-1-5458-1056-9 paperback edition
ISBN: 978-1-5458-1057-6 hardcover edition

Printed in China
October 2023

First Printing

MEET THE LOUD FAMILY *and friends!*

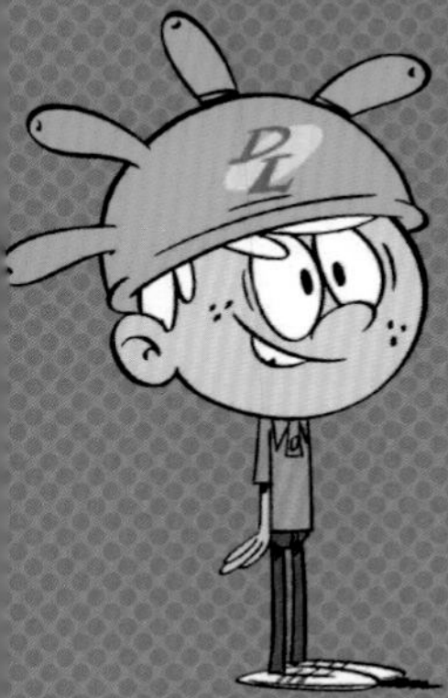

LINCOLN LOUD
THE MIDDLE CHILD

Lincoln is the middle child, with five older sisters and five younger sisters. He has learned that surviving the Loud household means staying a step ahead. As the "man with a plan," he's always coming up with a way to get what he wants or deal with a problem, even if things inevitably go wrong. But don't worry, Lincoln's got a backup plan for that, too. He loves comicbooks, video games, magic, fantasy and science fiction stories – all of which you might find him enjoying in his underwear. His favorite characters include secret agent David Steele (think James Bond), superhero Ace Savvy (think Superman with a knack for playing-card puns) and video game protagonist Muscle Fish.

He and his best friend Clyde make up the dynamic duo, Clincoln McCloud! They, along with his best friends (collectively known as "the Action News Team" because of the reporting they do for the school news program), always stick together – it's the best way to survive middle school.

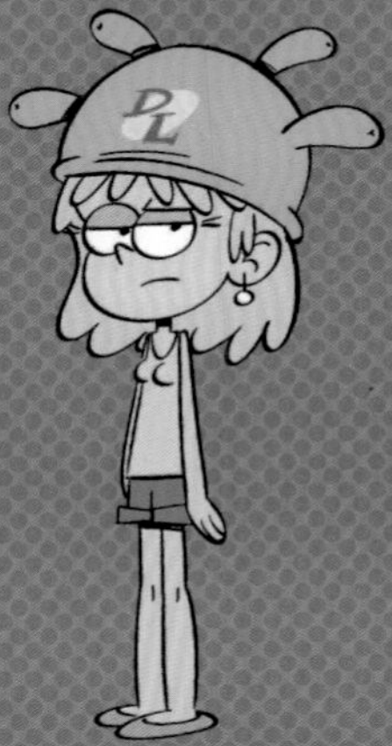

LORI LOUD
THE OLDEST

Lori's the first-born child of the Loud clan, and therefore sees herself as the boss of all her siblings. She feels she's paved the way for them and deserves extra respect. Her signature traits are rolling her eyes, texting her boyfriend Bobby (AKA "Boo-Boo Bear"), and literally saying "literally" all the time. Because she's the oldest and most experienced sibling, Lori can be a great ally, so it pays to stay on her good side, especially since she can drive.

Lori has begun attending Fairway University, a prestigious golf college, and is one of the youngest players to make the school's golf team. Even though she's moved away from home, she's always in touch with her siblings. Even at college, Lori is always part of the Loud family shenanigans.

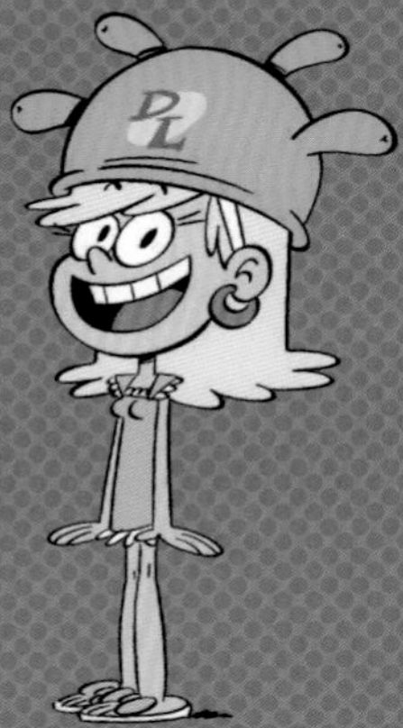

LENI LOUD
THE FASHIONISTA

Leni spends most of her time designing outfits, accessorizing, and shopping at the mall – which makes her the perfect sales employee at Reininger's department store. Her people-pleasing nature, natural leadership abilities, and fashion instincts keep customers coming back! Leni is supported by her best friends and co-workers, Miguel and Fiona (and sometimes Tanya the mannequin). And now she has the added support of her new boyfriend, Gavin, who works in the mall food court.

Back at the house, she always falls for Luan's pranks, and sometimes walks into walls when she's talking (she's not great at doing two things at once). But what Leni lacks in smarts, she makes up for in heart. She's the sweetest Loud around!

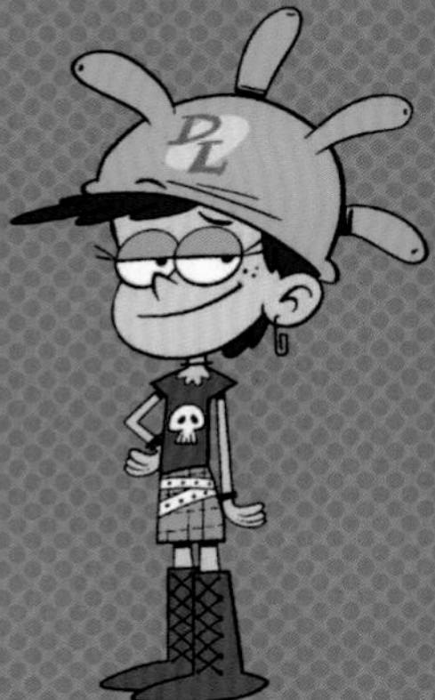

LUNA LOUD
THE ROCK STAR

Luna is loud, boisterous and freewheeling, and her energy is always cranked to 11. On the off-chance she doesn't have her guitar with her, everything can and will be turned into a musical instrument. You can always count on Luna to help out, and she'll do most anything you ask, as long as you're okay with her supplying a rocking musical accompaniment.

When she's not jamming, Luna is most likely hanging out with her girlfriend, Sam, or playing with their band, The Moon Goats. The two might even be found babysitting the McBride's cats – it turns out Sam's a natural cat whisperer!

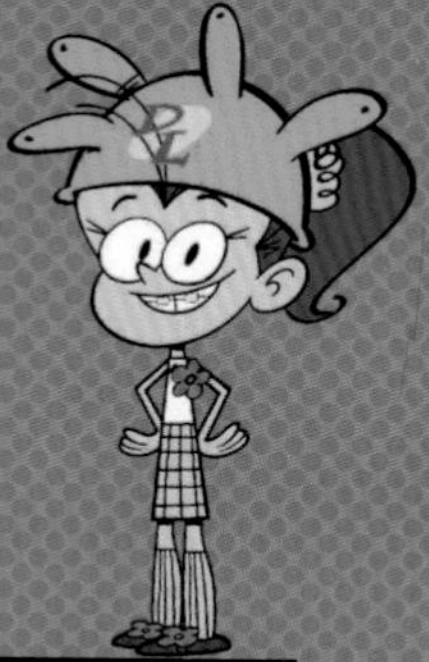

LUAN LOUD
THE JOKESTER

Luan is a standup comedienne who provides a nonstop barrage of silly puns. She's big on prop comedy – squirting flowers and whoopee cushions – so you have to be on your toes whenever she's around. She loves to pull pranks – April Fool's Day is her favorite day (and the rest of the Louds' least favorite). Luan is also a really good ventriloquist – she is often found doing bits with her dummy, Mr. Coconuts (but don't let him hear you calling him a "dummy"). At school, Luan and her boyfriend, Benny, are usually writing and performing in the high school's theatrical productions – under the somewhat melodramatic supervision of their drama teacher, Mrs. Bernardo. Luan has also reached new heights while playing Dairyland character Heidi Heifer during the theme park's season.

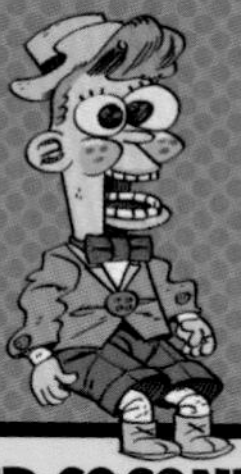

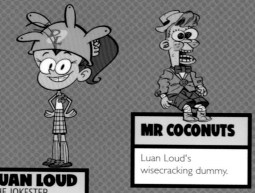

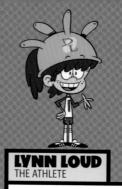

MR COCONUTS

Luan Loud's wisecracking dummy.

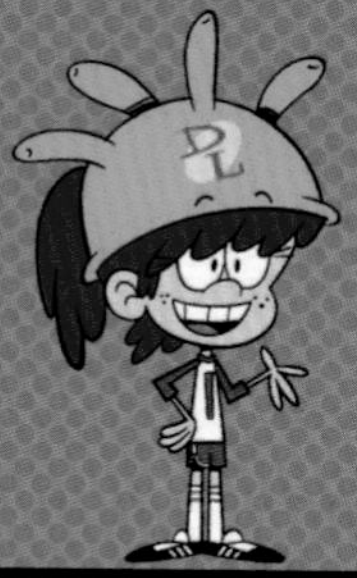

LYNN LOUD
THE ATHLETE

Lynn is athletic, full of energy, and always looking for a challenge or competition. She can turn anything into a sport. Putting away eggs? Jump shot! Score! Cleaning up the eggs? Slap shot! Score! Despite her competitive nature, Lynn always tries to have a good time with her family... and her teammates and best friends Paula and Margo. At school, she takes her duties as hall monitor seriously and doesn't tolerate any slackers... but she also shows a lot of heart when looking after Lincoln in his first year at middle school. One super fun fact about Lynn: her name is really Lynn Jr. (L.J.), because she's named after Dad!

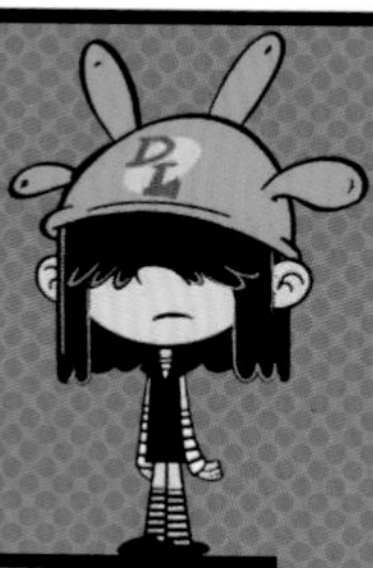

LUCY LOUD
THE EMO

Lucy can always be counted on to give the morbid point of view in any given situation. She is obsessed with all things spooky and dark – funerals, vampires, séances... you get the idea. Lucy has a way of mysteriously appearing out of nowhere, and try as they might, her siblings never get used to this. She loves the character of Edwin from the TV show "Vampires of Melancholia," and has a homemade bust of him hidden in her closet.

Lucy spends most of her time with her friends in the Morticians Club, of which she's a co-president. Together, the club speaks to spirits, attends casket conventions, and rides around in a hearse (well, technically it's just a station wagon painted black). Their motto is "Keep Calm and Embalm."

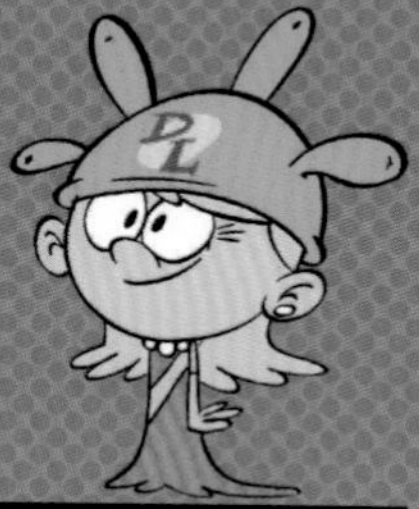

LOLA LOUD
THE BEAUTY QUEEN

Lola is a pageant powerhouse whose interests include glitter, photo shoots, and her own beautiful, beautiful face. But don't let her cute, gap-toothed smile fool you; underneath all the sugar and spice lurks a Machiavellian mastermind. Whatever Lola wants, Lola gets – or else. She's the eyes and ears of the household and never resists an opportunity to tattle on troublemakers. But if you stay on Lola's good side, you've got yourself a fierce ally – and a credit line to the first national bank of Lola. She might even let you drive her around in her pink jeep while she practices her pageant wave.

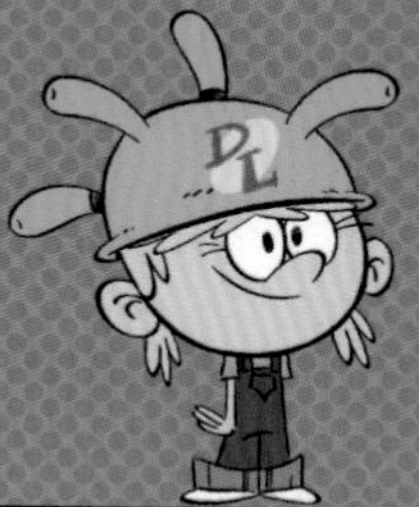

LANA LOUD
THE TOMBOY

Lana is the rough-and-tumble sparkplug counterpart to her twin sister, Lola. She's all about animals, mud pies, and muffler repairs. She's the resident Ms. Fix-it and animal whisperer, and is always ready to lend a hand – the dirtier the job, the better. Need your toilet unclogged? Snake trained? Back-zit popped? Lana's your gal. All she asks in return is a handful of kibble (she often sneaks it from the dog bowl anyway) or anything you can fish out of a nearby garbage can. She's proud of who she is, and her big heart definitely overpowers her pungent dumpster smell. Needless to say, while the twins love each other deep down, they've been known to get into some pretty epic brawls, mud and sequins flying. But when they join forces (like the time they pretended to be each other for their own personal gain), the rest of the Louds had better look out.

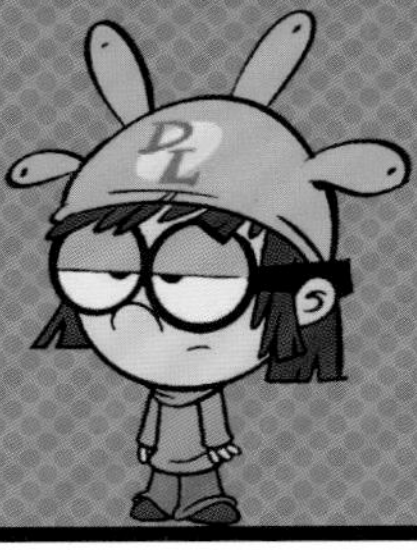

LISA LOUD
THE GENIUS

Lisa is smarter than the rest of her siblings combined, which would still be big news even if she wasn't only four years old. Lisa spends most of her time working in her bedroom lab (the family has gotten used to the explosions), and says her research leaves little time for frivolous pursuits like "playing" or "human interaction." Despite this, she can still find time to unwind with a little bit of West Coast rap. She has a collection of robot companions that she's created over the years, but these days relies mostly on Todd, her newest (and sassiest) mechanical friend. Together they've traveled back in time, launched themselves into outer space, and enjoyed many hours watching Todd's favorite TV show, "Robot Dance Party." At school (where Lisa is smarter than her teacher), she is learning to enjoy social interaction with her friend Darcy, but will forego nap time to work on all the top secret projects she's got going on with the Norwegian government.

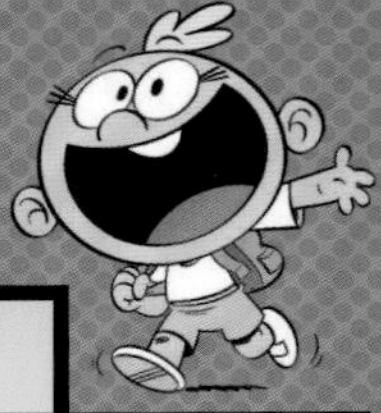

LILY LOUD
THE BABY

Lily's the baby of the family, but she's growing up fast. She's a toddler now and can speak full sentences– well, sometimes. As an infant she was already mischievous, but now she's upped her game. Her most important goal – other than tricking the family into taking her for ice cream – is to impress the other preschool kids at show and tell. No matter what, though, she still brings a smile to everyone's faces, and the family loves her unconditionally.

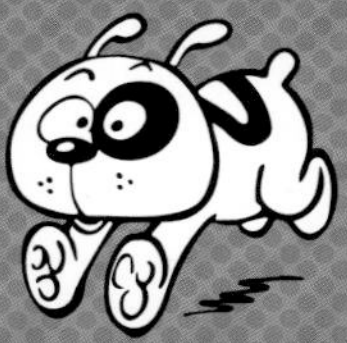

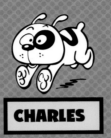

CHARLES

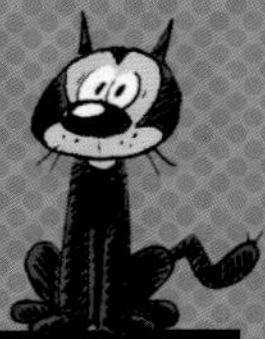

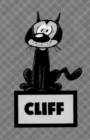

CLIFF

RITA LOUD

Mother to the eleven Loud kids, Mom Rita wears many different hats. She's a chauffeur, homework-checker and barf cleaner-upper all rolled into one. Mom is organized and keeps the family running like a well-oiled machine. She's always there for her kids and ready to jump into action during a crisis, whether it's a fight between the twins or finding Leni's missing shoe. When she's not chasing the kids, she's a columnist for the Royal Woods Gazette. As a skilled writer, she's able to connect with her readers as a mom simply trying to do her best. She also loves taking on house projects and is very handy with tools (guess that's where Lana gets it from). Between writing her novel, working on her column, and being a mom, her days are always hectic - but she wouldn't have it any other way.

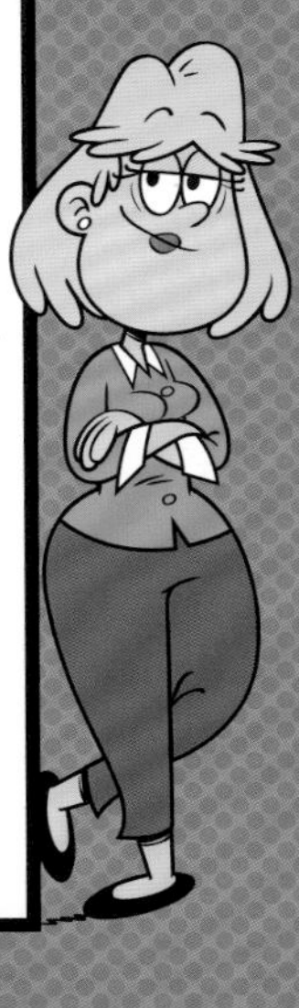

LYNN LOUD SR.

Dad (Lynn Loud Sr.) is a fun-loving, upbeat chef and owner of Lynn's Table – a family style restaurant that specializes in serving delicious but outrageously named meals like Lynn-sagna and Lynn-ger chicken. A sentimental kid-at-heart, he's not above taking part in the kids' zany schemes but is more well known for the emotions he wears on his sleeves: his sobbing – both for joy and sadness – is legendary. In addition to cooking, Dad loves his van (affectionately named Vanzilla), British culture, and making puns with any of the kids not already rolling their eyes. Most of all, Dad loves rocking out with his best friend and head waiter, Kotaro. They're part of a cowbell-focused band with some other dads in Royal Woods; hence their band name: The Doo-Dads.

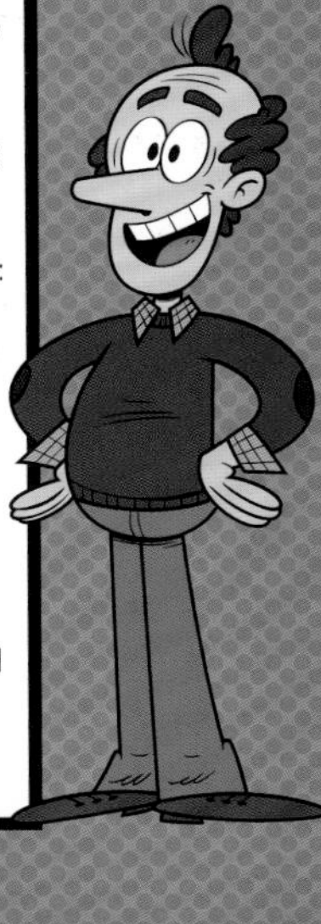
DL

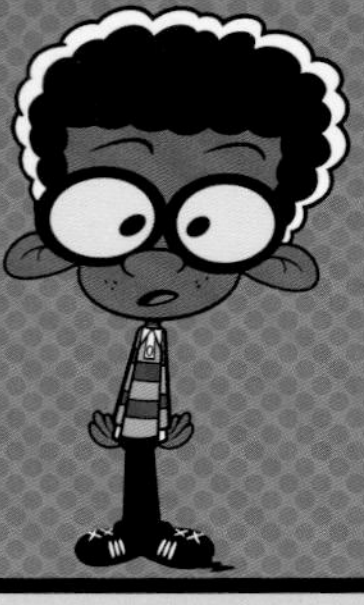

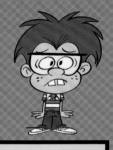

CLYDE McBRIDE

Clyde is Lincoln's best friend in the whole world… so it probably goes without saying that he's also Lincoln's partner in crime. Clyde is always willing to go along with Lincoln's crazy schemes, even if he sees the flaws in them up-front or if they sometimes give him anxiety tummy aches. Lincoln and Clyde are two peas in a pod and share pretty much all of the same tastes in movies, comics, TV shows, toys—you name it. Clyde knows exactly who he is and is not afraid to show it! As an only child, Clyde envies Lincoln—how cool would it be to always have siblings around to talk to? But since Clyde spends so much time at the Loud house, he's almost an honorary sibling anyway. Clyde is a little neurotic, but that's probably because he's the son of helicopter dads, Howard and Harold. They are VERY over-protective and VERY involved in his life. Clyde isn't spoiled, he's just extremely well-cared for. But he's slowly learning to stand on his own two feet and his dads are starting to see how well he can take care of himself.

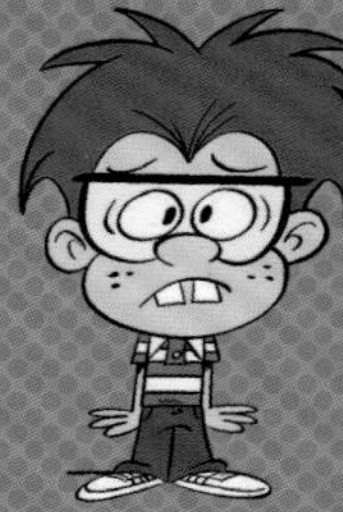

ZACH GURDLE

Lincoln's pal Zach is a self-admitted nerd who's obsessed with aliens and conspiracy theories. (He's just following in the footsteps of his alien hunting parents.) Zach lives between a freeway and a circus, so the chaos of the Loud House doesn't faze him. To Zach, everything is a mystery to be solved or coverup to be exposed. His best friend in the gang is Rusty, with whom he occasionally butts heads. But deep down, it's all love.

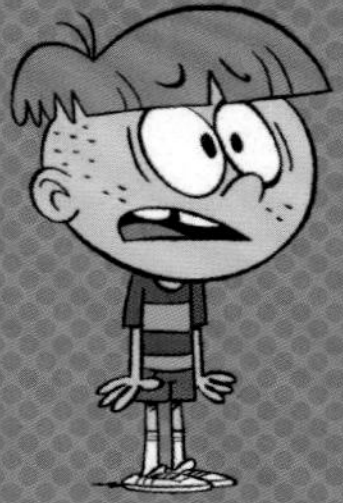

LIAM HUNNICUTT

Lincoln's friend Liam is an enthusiastic, sweet-natured farm boy full of down-home wisdom. He loves hanging out with his Mee Maw, wrestling his prize pig Virginia, and sharing his farm-to-table produce with the rest of the gang. No matter the situation, Liam faces it with optimism.

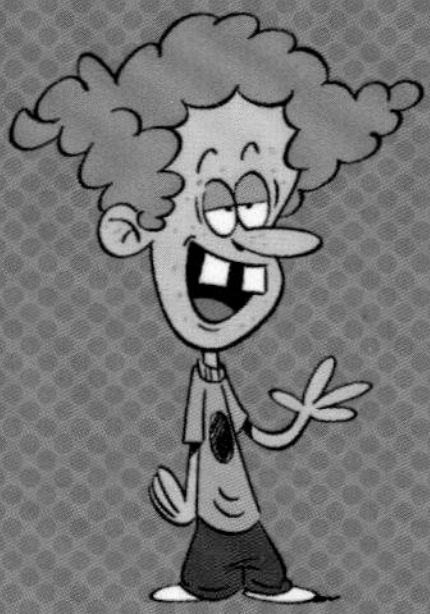

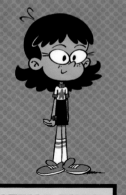

RUSTY SPOKES

Lincoln's friend Rusty is a self-proclaimed ladies' man who's always the first to dish out girl advice— even though he's never been on an actual date. No one has more confidence than Rusty, even if that confidence is often completely misguided. Rusty's a looker – at least in his own eyes – and is always working hard to protect his face (what he calls his "moneymaker"). Rusty is always sharing advice from his experienced but equally delusional cousin, Derek. No matter what the situation, it seems like Derek's been there before and lived to tell about it. Rusty's dad, Rodney, owns a clothing store called "Duds for Dudes," so he can always hook the gang up with some dapper duds—just as long as no one gets anything dirty.

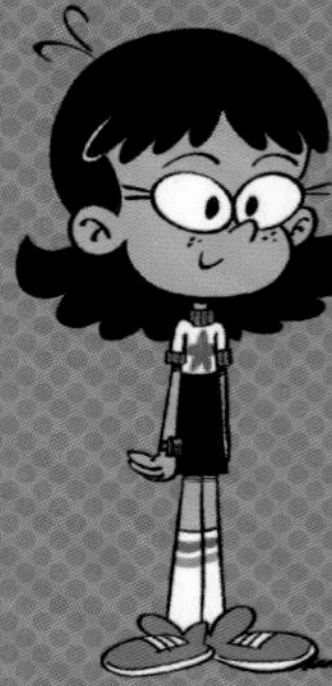

STELLA ZHAU

Lincoln's pal Stella is a tech genius, always building new devices – usually from parts she's salvaged from old devices. She loves to take things apart just to see how they work. Her smarts help keep the gang focused and on track, especially when they're chasing a news story. Stella will happily take charge of a situation – she's helped solve many a school mystery and even improved the gang's shield formation defense in dodgeball.

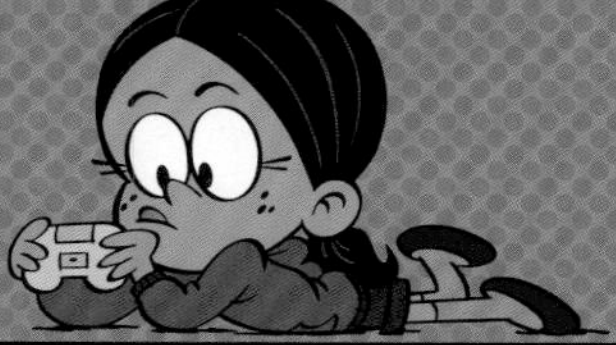

RONNIE ANNE SANTIAGO

Ronnie Anne's a skateboarding city girl now. She's fearless, free-spirited, and always quick to come up with a plan. She's one tough cookie, but she also has a sweet side. Ronnie Anne loves helping her family, and that's taught her to help others too. When she's not pitching in at the family *mercado*, you can find her exploring the neighborhood with her best friend Sid, or ordering hot dogs with her skater buds Casey, Nikki, and Sameer. Having a family as big as the Casagrandes has taught Ronnie Anne to deal with anything life throws her way.

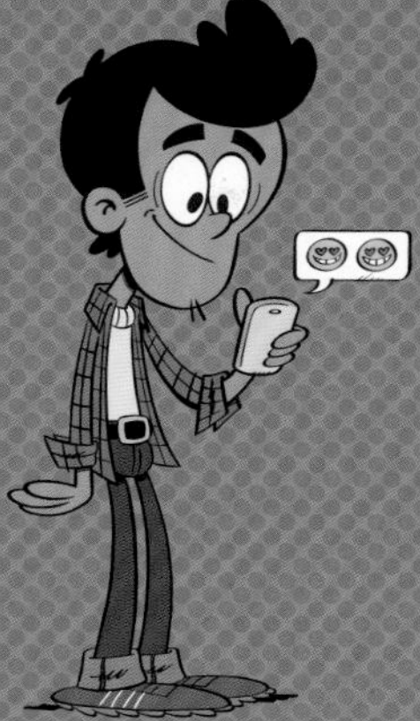

BOBBY SANTIAGO

Bobby is Ronnie Anne's big bro. He's a student and one of the hardest workers in the city. He loves his family and loves working at the *mercado*. As his *abuelo's* right hand man, Bobby can't wait to take over the family business one day. He's a big kid at heart, and his clumsiness gets him into some sticky situations at work, like locking himself in the freezer. *Mercado* mishaps aside, everyone in the neighborhood loves to come to the store and talk to Bobby.

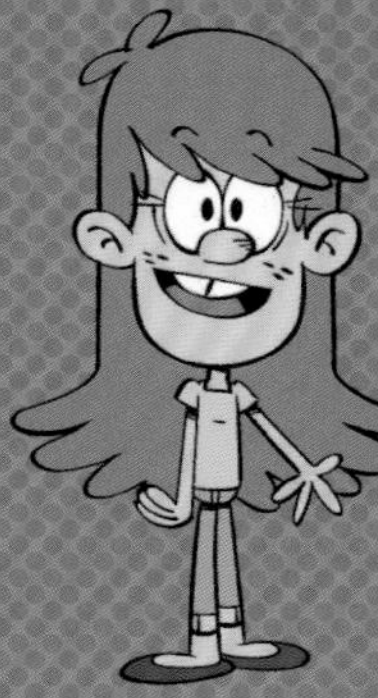

MARGO

Margo is Lynn's best friend and teammate, and a fellow sports fan. She shares Lynn's passion for greasy food and never turns down a trip to the Burpin' Burger. Margo is enthusiastic and energetic, but also tends to be easy-going and humble. She's a great friend to Lynn and always supportive of her.

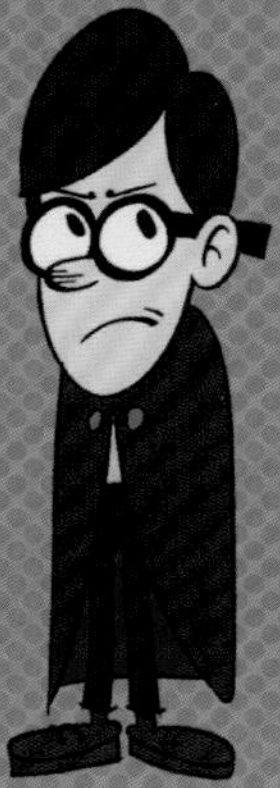

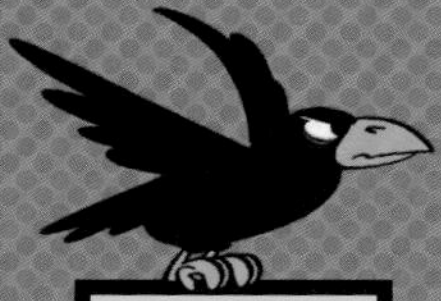

THORN

MORPHEUS

Morpheus is the snarkiest member of the Morticians Club. He believes that just because you're somber and gloomy, it doesn't mean you can't also be ready with a saucy quip. Morpheus' best friend is his crow, Thorn.

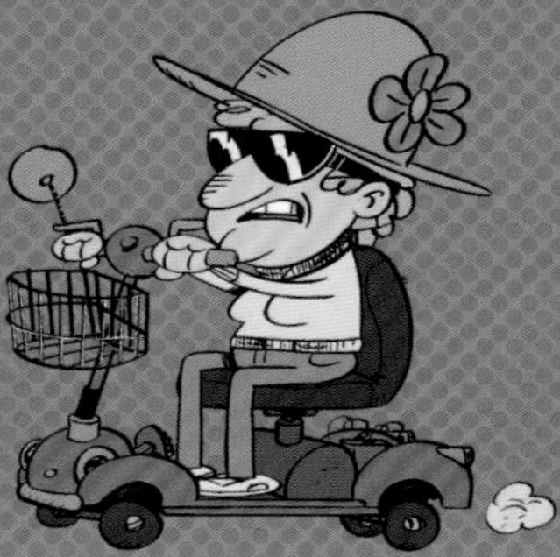

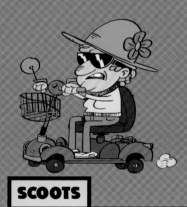

SCOOTS

Every town has its outspoken, cranky busybody, and in Royal Woods that person is Scoots. The words "no nonsense" were definitely created with her in mind. Whether she's terrorizing pedestrians with her motorized scooter, or eating all the pudding in the cafeteria at Sunset Canyon, Scoots makes it clear that it's her world and everyone else is just living in it.

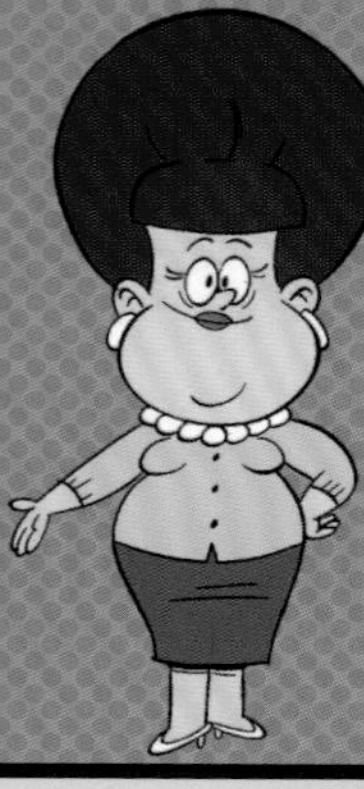

CHERYL FARRELL

Cheryl is the secretary at Royal Woods Elementary School and identical twin to Meryl, who lovingly calls her "Cher-Bear!" She is a bubbly Southerner who is always rooting for the students at Royal Woods Elementary. She loves boot scootin', storing items in her signature beehive hairdo, and watching soap operas with her sister in their shared condo.

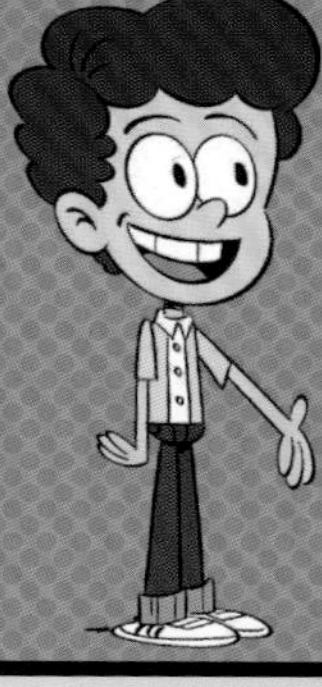

BENNY STEIN

Benny is Luan's classmate, co-star and, most importantly, boyfriend. He's shy and quirky, but also sweet and earnest. He's not a zany comedian like Luan, but he sure enjoys her sense of humor and appreciates her wicked skills when it comes to prop comedy. Whenever he's too shy to speak for himself, he speaks through his ventriloquist's dummy, Mrs. Appleblossom—who has a Mrs. Doubtfire-esque British accent.

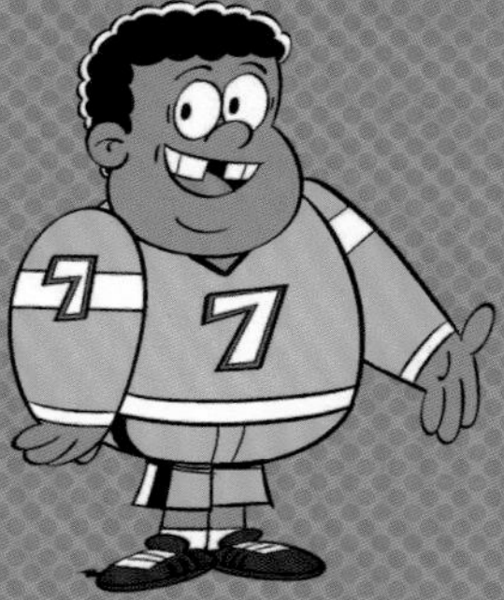

SPENCER

Spencer is another classmate of Luan's and part of the Royal Woods High School drama department. Unlike Shannon, however, he's super happy with any role he gets, be it "announcer guy" or "clown judge number three." The adage "there are no small parts" was definitely created with Spencer in mind.

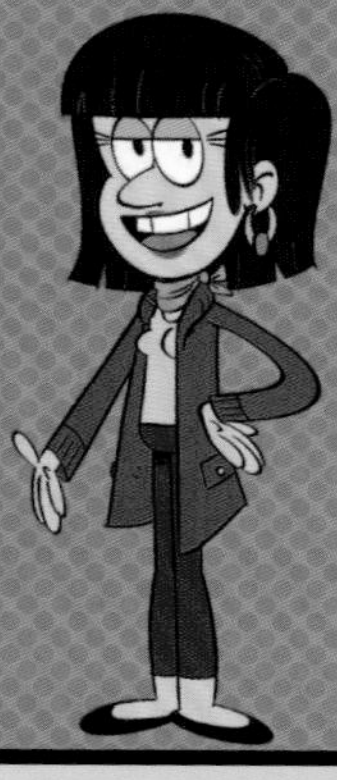

MRS. BERNARDO

Kate Bernardo is Luan and Benny's drama teacher at Royal Woods Middle School. And she's well-suited for the job, since no one is more dramatic than her. Every moment of her life is performed to the hilt, with abundant (and exhausting) flair and flourishes. Mrs. B is always performing a new one-woman show, covering scintillating topics like the time her waitress application at Dad's restaurant was rejected, and touting her extensive acting resume, including her prized role as "nervous customer number one" in a TV commercial that only aired once on a late night cable show.

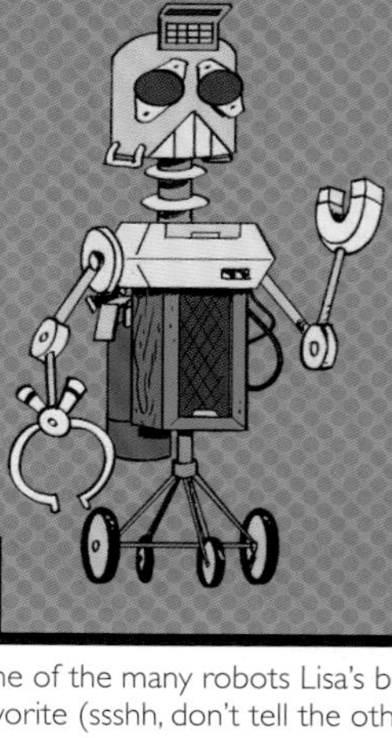

TODD BOT

While Todd is just one of the many robots Lisa's built, he's definitely her favorite (ssshh, don't tell the others!). He's outspoken and opinionated, and sometimes a little too sassy for Lisa (which is why she installed a button to dial down the sassiness). Still, she relies on him for everything, from coordinating scientific presentations worldwide, to building rockets and time travel devices, to providing a funky beat she can rap to. Todd is a loyal companion to Lisa - except, you know, when someone accidentally flips his "villain" switch, and then he just wants to destroy Royal Woods (but this rarely happens so it's all good).

"TALL ENOUGH"

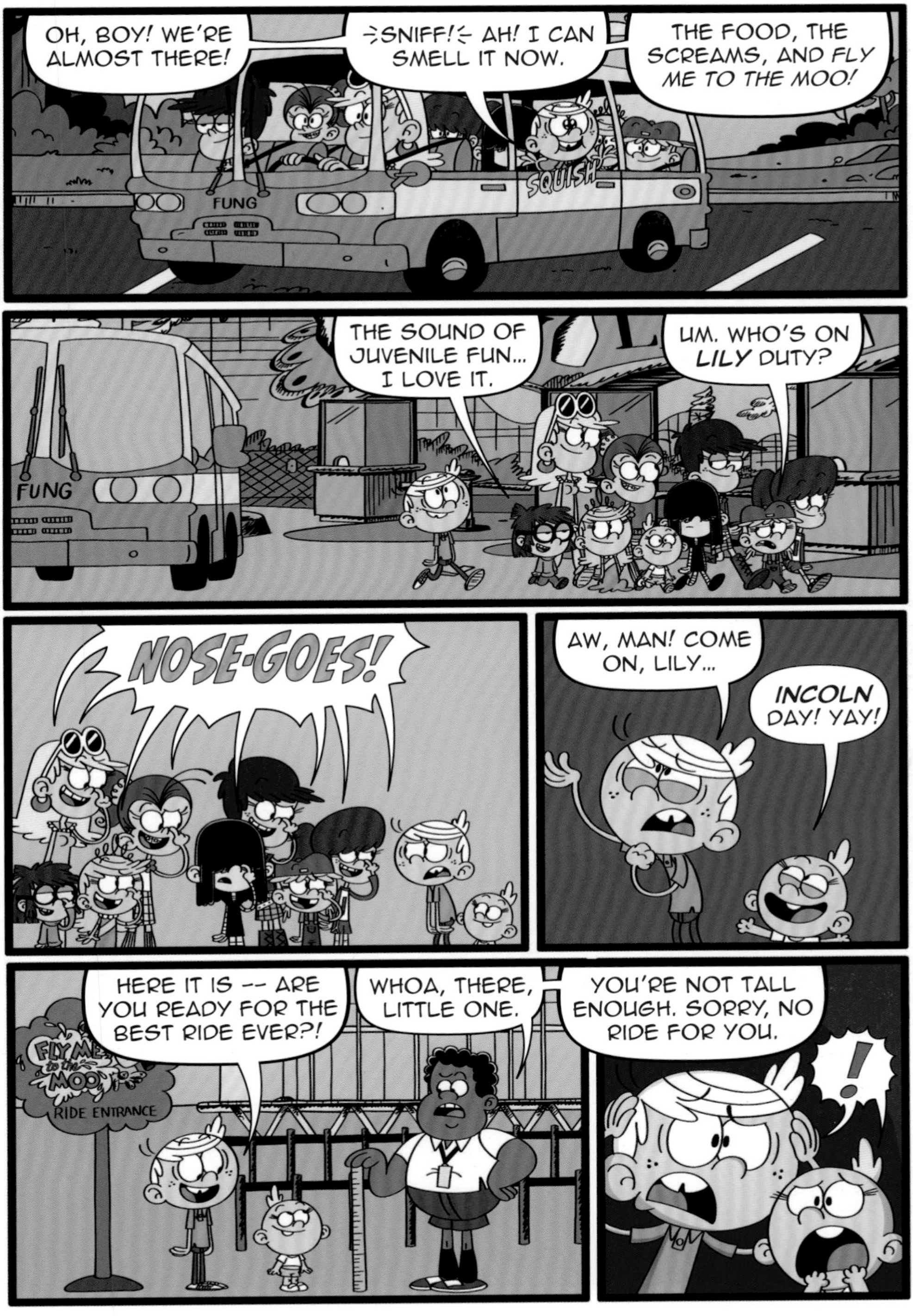

OH, BOY! WE'RE ALMOST THERE!
SNIFF! AH! I CAN SMELL IT NOW.
THE FOOD, THE SCREAMS, AND FLY ME TO THE MOO!
FUNG
SQUISH
THE SOUND OF JUVENILE FUN... I LOVE IT.
UM. WHO'S ON LILY DUTY?
FUNG
NOSE-GOES!
AW, MAN! COME ON, LILY...
INCOLN DAY! YAY!
HERE IT IS -- ARE YOU READY FOR THE BEST RIDE EVER?!
FLY ME to the MOO
RIDE ENTRANCE
WHOA, THERE, LITTLE ONE.
YOU'RE NOT TALL ENOUGH. SORRY, NO RIDE FOR YOU.
!

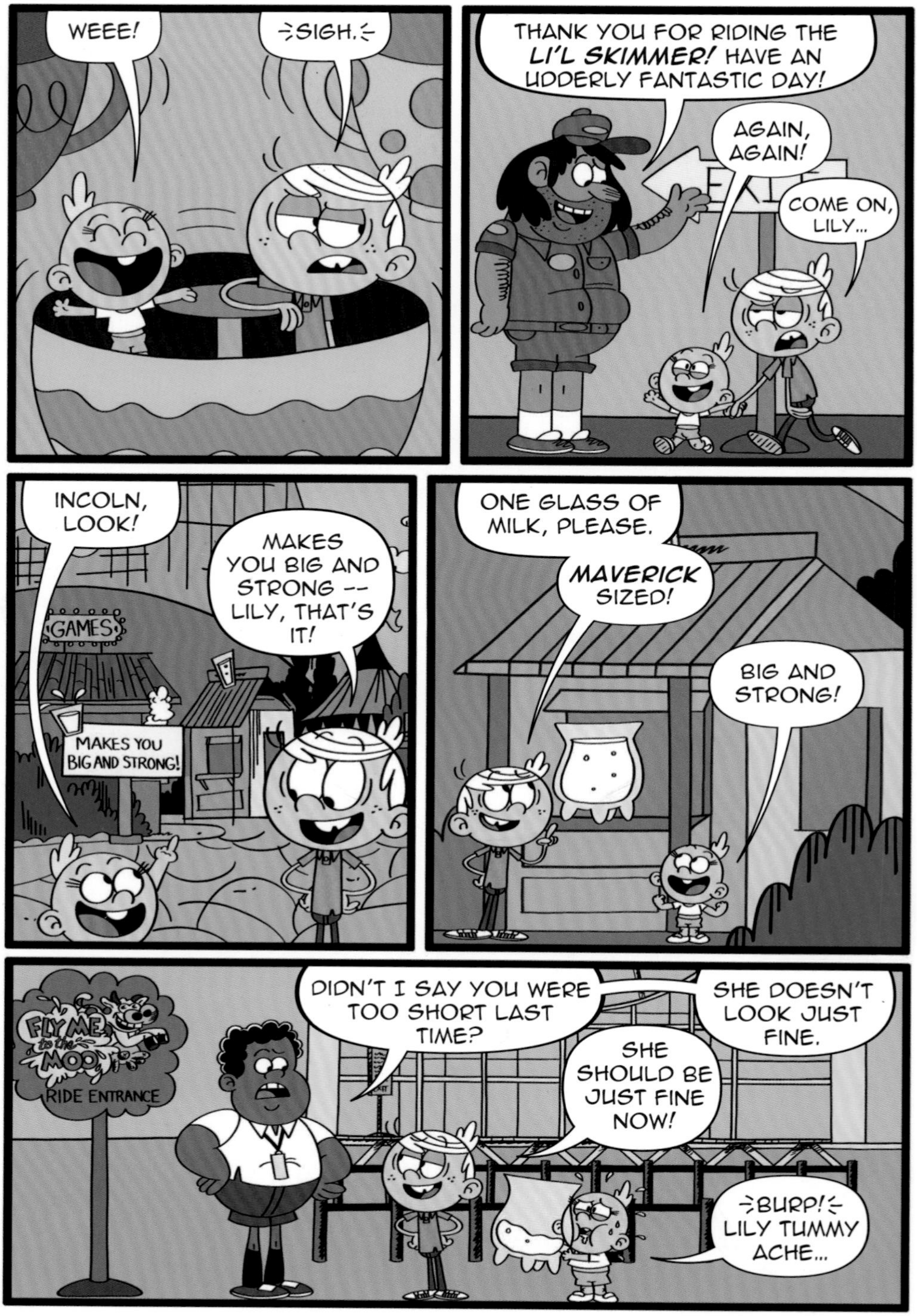
WEEE!
SIGH.
THANK YOU FOR RIDING THE LI'L SKIMMER! HAVE AN UDDERLY FANTASTIC DAY!
AGAIN, AGAIN!
COME ON, LILY...
INCOLN, LOOK!
GAMES
MAKES YOU BIG AND STRONG!
MAKES YOU BIG AND STRONG -- LILY, THAT'S IT!
ONE GLASS OF MILK, PLEASE.
MAVERICK SIZED!
BIG AND STRONG!
FLY ME to the MOO
RIDE ENTRANCE
DIDN'T I SAY YOU WERE TOO SHORT LAST TIME?
SHE SHOULD BE JUST FINE NOW!
SHE DOESN'T LOOK JUST FINE.
BURP! LILY TUMMY ACHE...

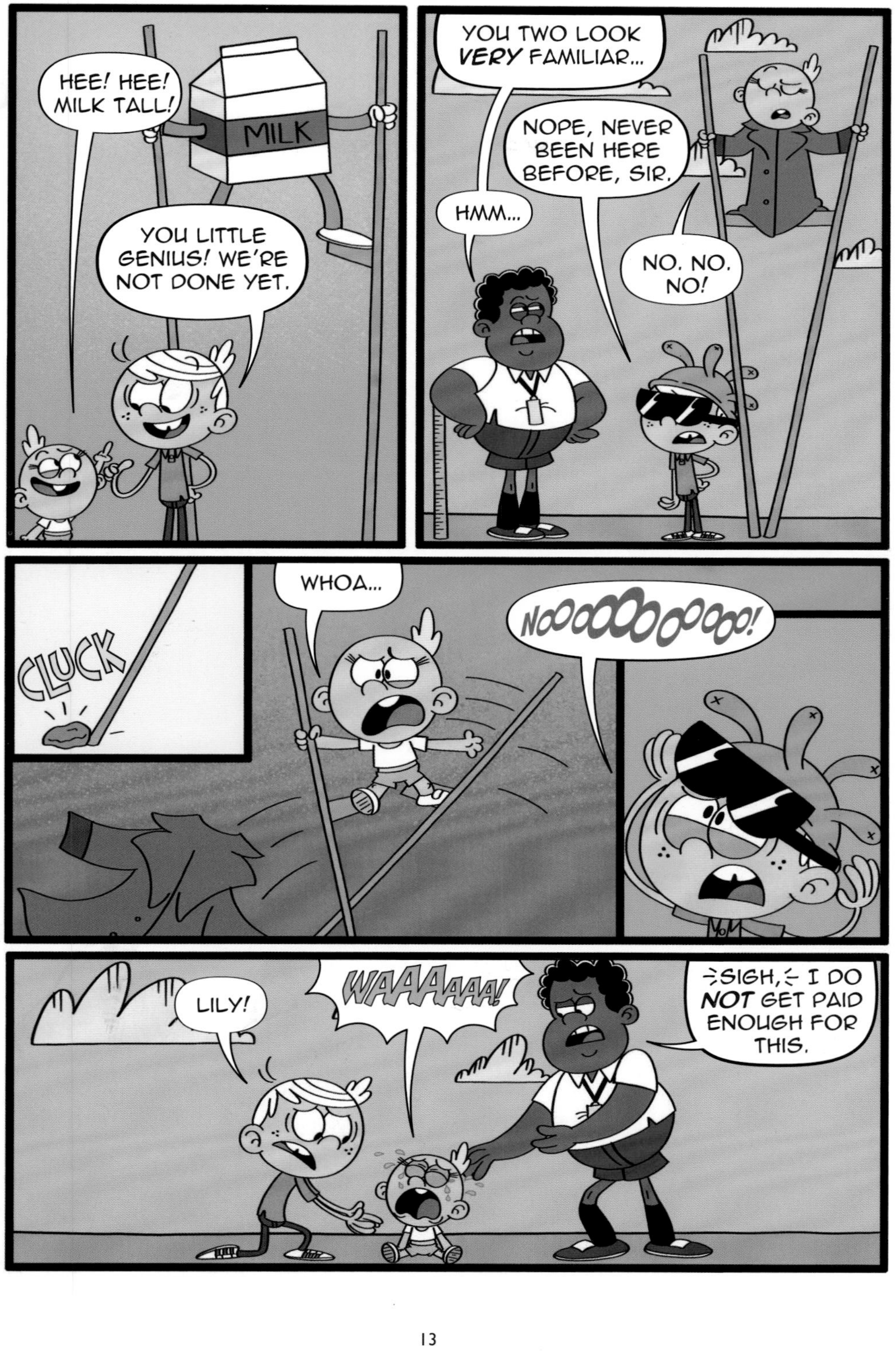
HEE! HEE! MILK TALL!
MILK
YOU LITTLE GENIUS! WE'RE NOT DONE YET.
YOU TWO LOOK **VERY** FAMILIAR...
NOPE, NEVER BEEN HERE BEFORE, SIR.
HMM...
NO. NO. NO!
CLUCK
WHOA...
NOOOOOOOOOOO!
LILY!
WAAAAAAA!
SIGH, I DO **NOT** GET PAID ENOUGH FOR THIS.

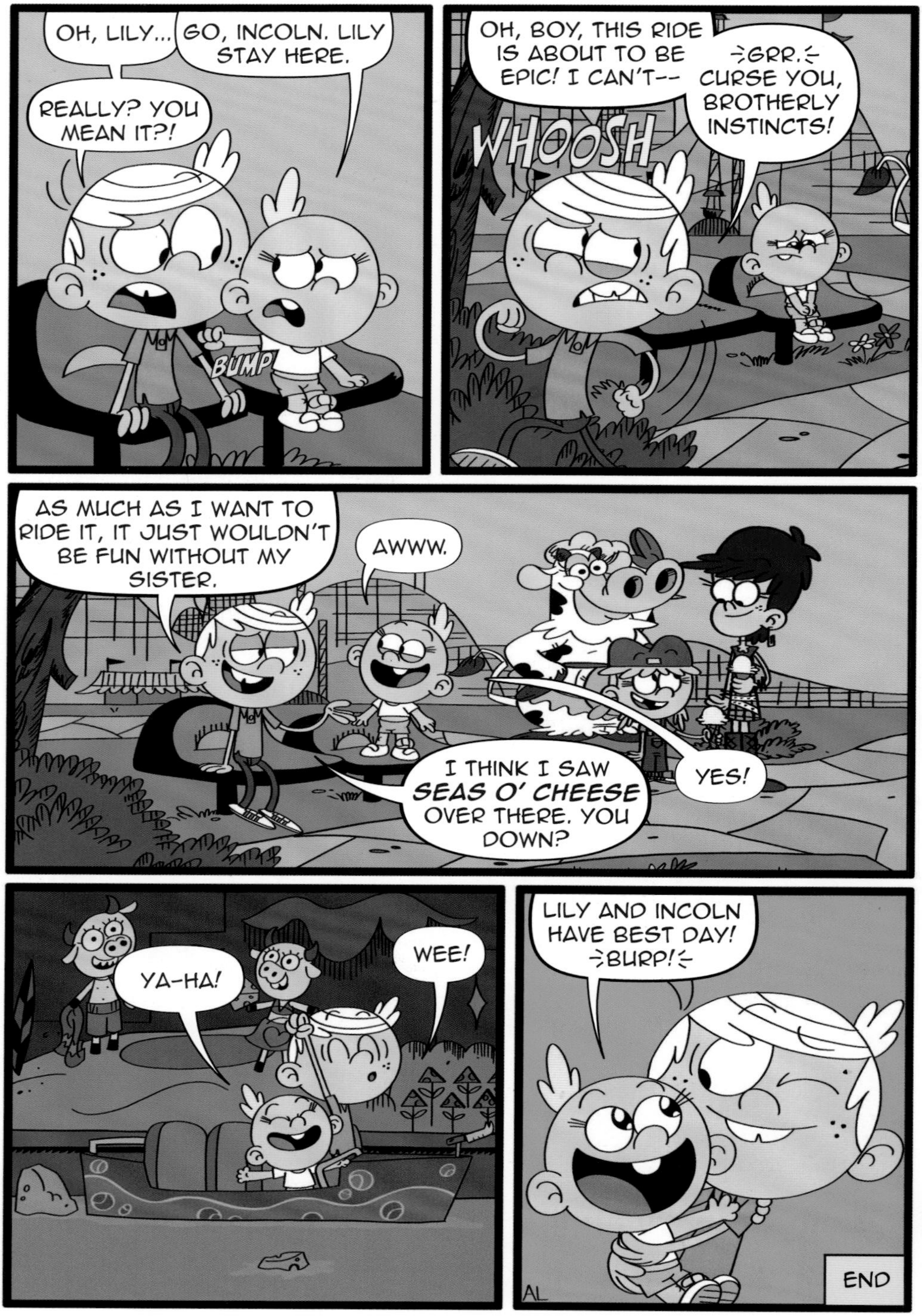

OH, LILY...
GO, INCOLN. LILY STAY HERE.
REALLY? YOU MEAN IT?!
BUMP
OH, BOY, THIS RIDE IS ABOUT TO BE EPIC! I CAN'T--
GRR. CURSE YOU, BROTHERLY INSTINCTS!
WHOOSH
AS MUCH AS I WANT TO RIDE IT, IT JUST WOULDN'T BE FUN WITHOUT MY SISTER.
AWWW.
I THINK I SAW SEAS O' CHEESE OVER THERE. YOU DOWN?
YES!
YA-HA!
WEE!
LILY AND INCOLN HAVE BEST DAY! BURP!
AL
END

"DON'T BE A DRAG"

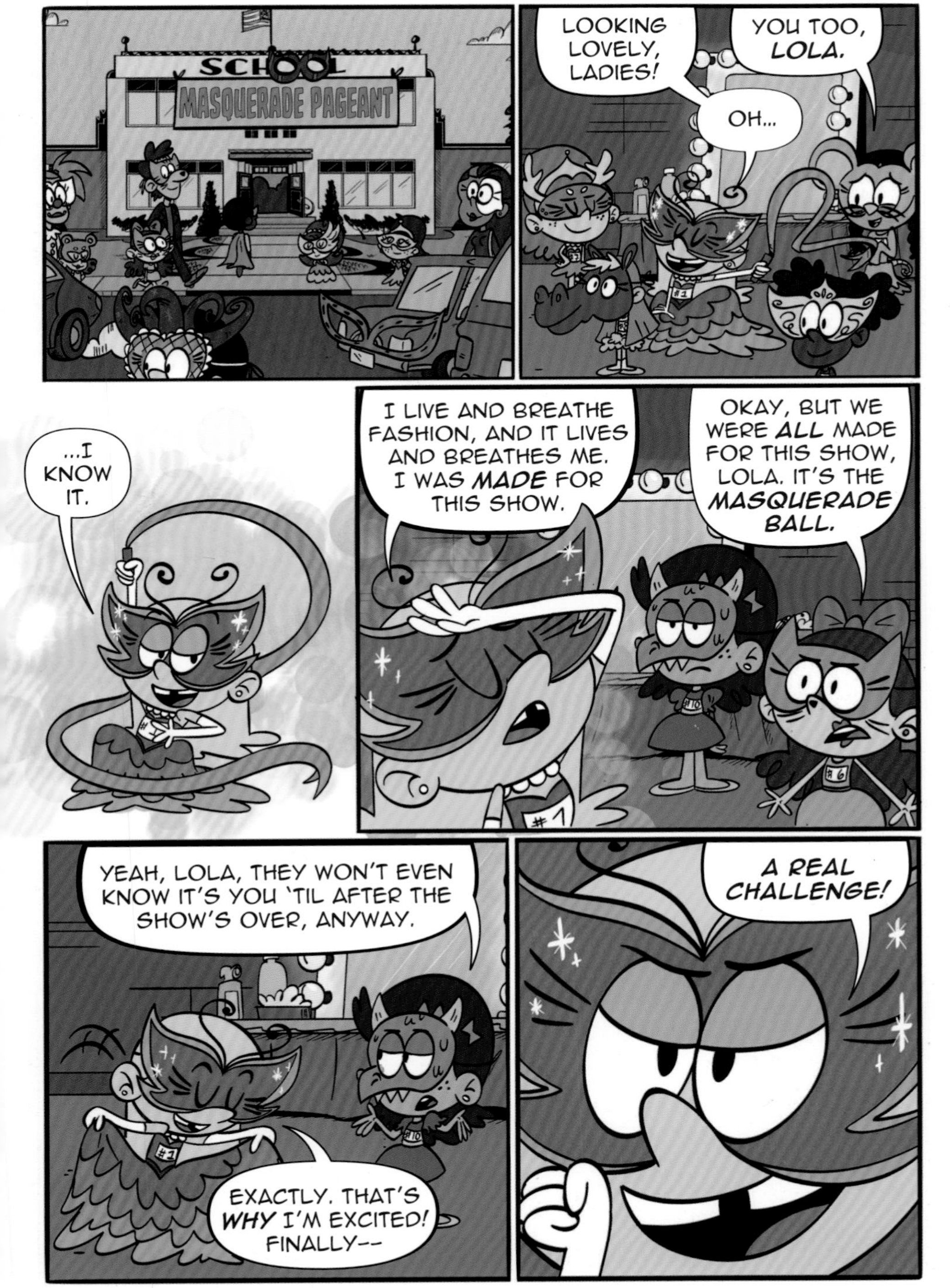

SCHOOL
MASQUERADE PAGEANT
LOOKING LOVELY, LADIES!
YOU TOO, *LOLA.*
OH...
...I KNOW IT.
I LIVE AND BREATHE FASHION, AND IT LIVES AND BREATHES ME. I WAS *MADE* FOR THIS SHOW.
OKAY, BUT WE WERE *ALL* MADE FOR THIS SHOW, LOLA. IT'S THE *MASQUERADE BALL.*
YEAH, LOLA, THEY WON'T EVEN KNOW IT'S YOU 'TIL AFTER THE SHOW'S OVER, ANYWAY.
EXACTLY. THAT'S *WHY* I'M EXCITED! FINALLY--
A REAL CHALLENGE!

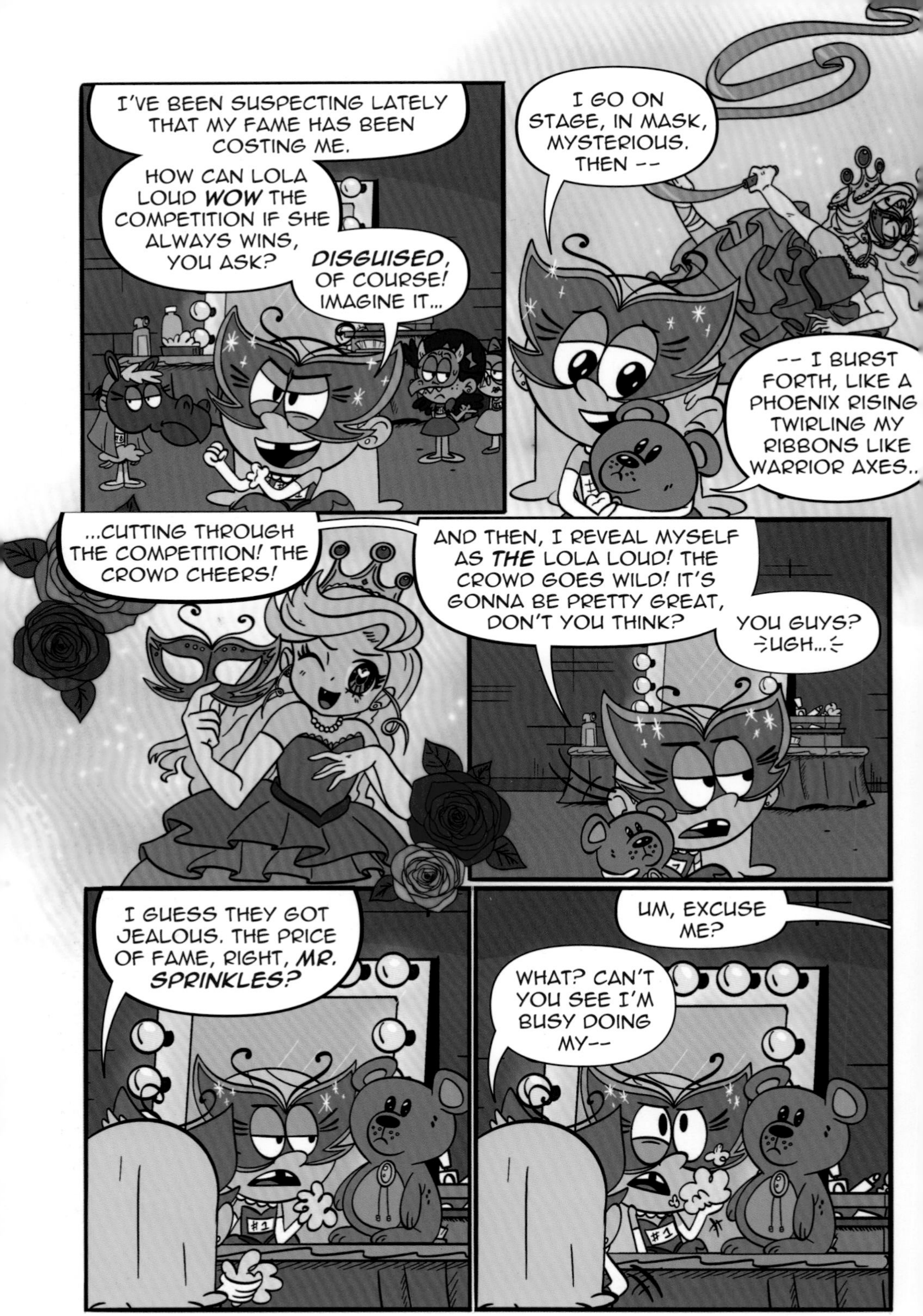
I'VE BEEN SUSPECTING LATELY THAT MY FAME HAS BEEN COSTING ME.
HOW CAN LOLA LOUD **WOW** THE COMPETITION IF SHE ALWAYS WINS, YOU ASK?
DISGUISED, OF COURSE! IMAGINE IT...
I GO ON STAGE, IN MASK, MYSTERIOUS. THEN --
-- I BURST FORTH, LIKE A PHOENIX RISING TWIRLING MY RIBBONS LIKE WARRIOR AXES...
...CUTTING THROUGH THE COMPETITION! THE CROWD CHEERS!
AND THEN, I REVEAL MYSELF AS ***THE*** LOLA LOUD! THE CROWD GOES WILD! IT'S GONNA BE PRETTY GREAT, DON'T YOU THINK?
YOU GUYS?
UGH...
I GUESS THEY GOT JEALOUS. THE PRICE OF FAME, RIGHT, ***MR. SPRINKLES?***
UM, EXCUSE ME?
WHAT? CAN'T YOU SEE I'M BUSY DOING MY--

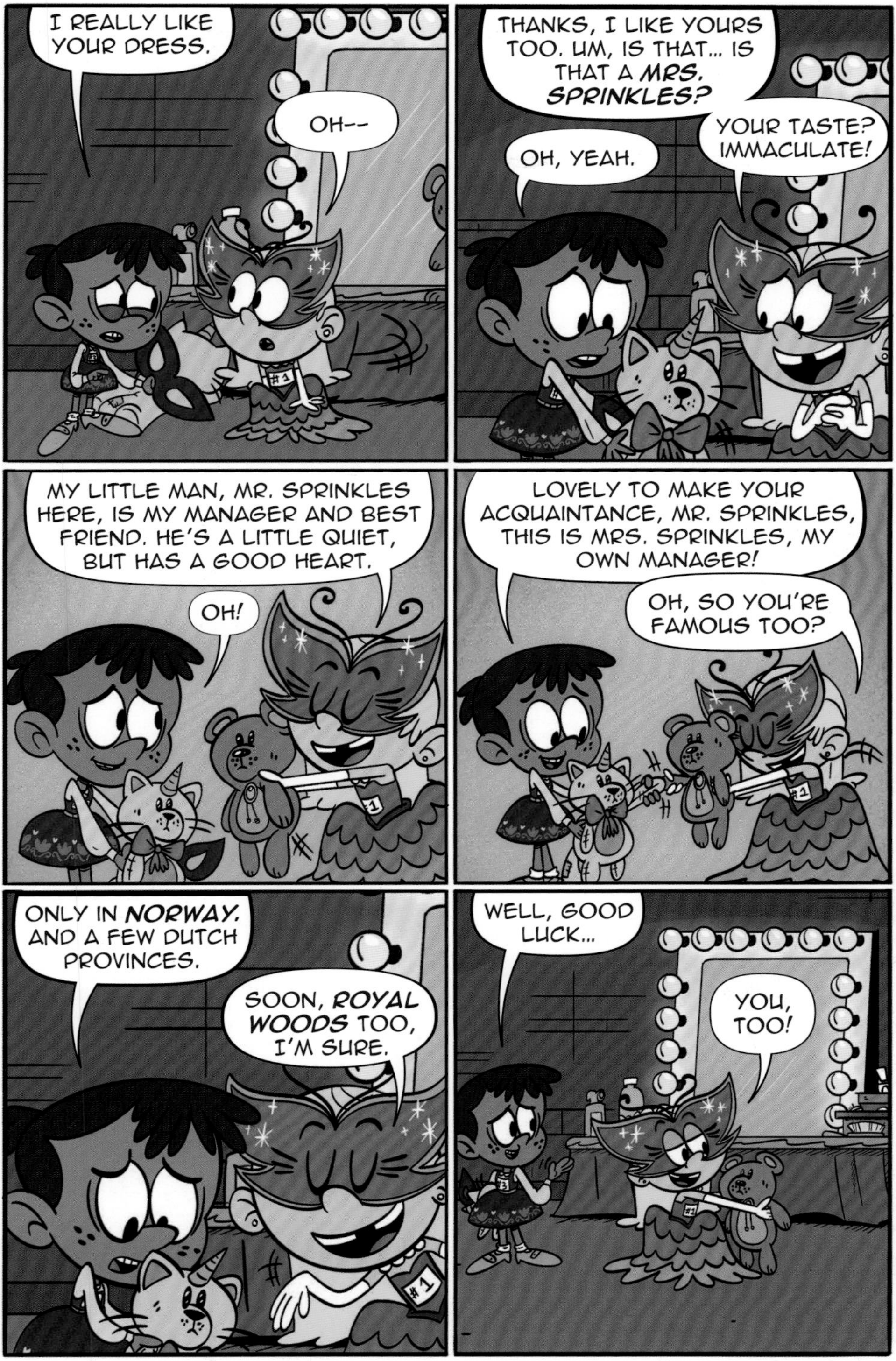
I REALLY LIKE YOUR DRESS.
OH--
THANKS, I LIKE YOURS TOO. UM, IS THAT... IS THAT A ***MRS. SPRINKLES?***
OH, YEAH.
YOUR TASTE? IMMACULATE!
MY LITTLE MAN, MR. SPRINKLES HERE, IS MY MANAGER AND BEST FRIEND. HE'S A LITTLE QUIET, BUT HAS A GOOD HEART.
OH!
LOVELY TO MAKE YOUR ACQUAINTANCE, MR. SPRINKLES, THIS IS MRS. SPRINKLES, MY OWN MANAGER!
OH, SO YOU'RE FAMOUS TOO?
ONLY IN ***NORWAY.*** AND A FEW DUTCH PROVINCES.
SOON, ***ROYAL WOODS*** TOO, I'M SURE.
WELL, GOOD LUCK...
YOU, TOO!

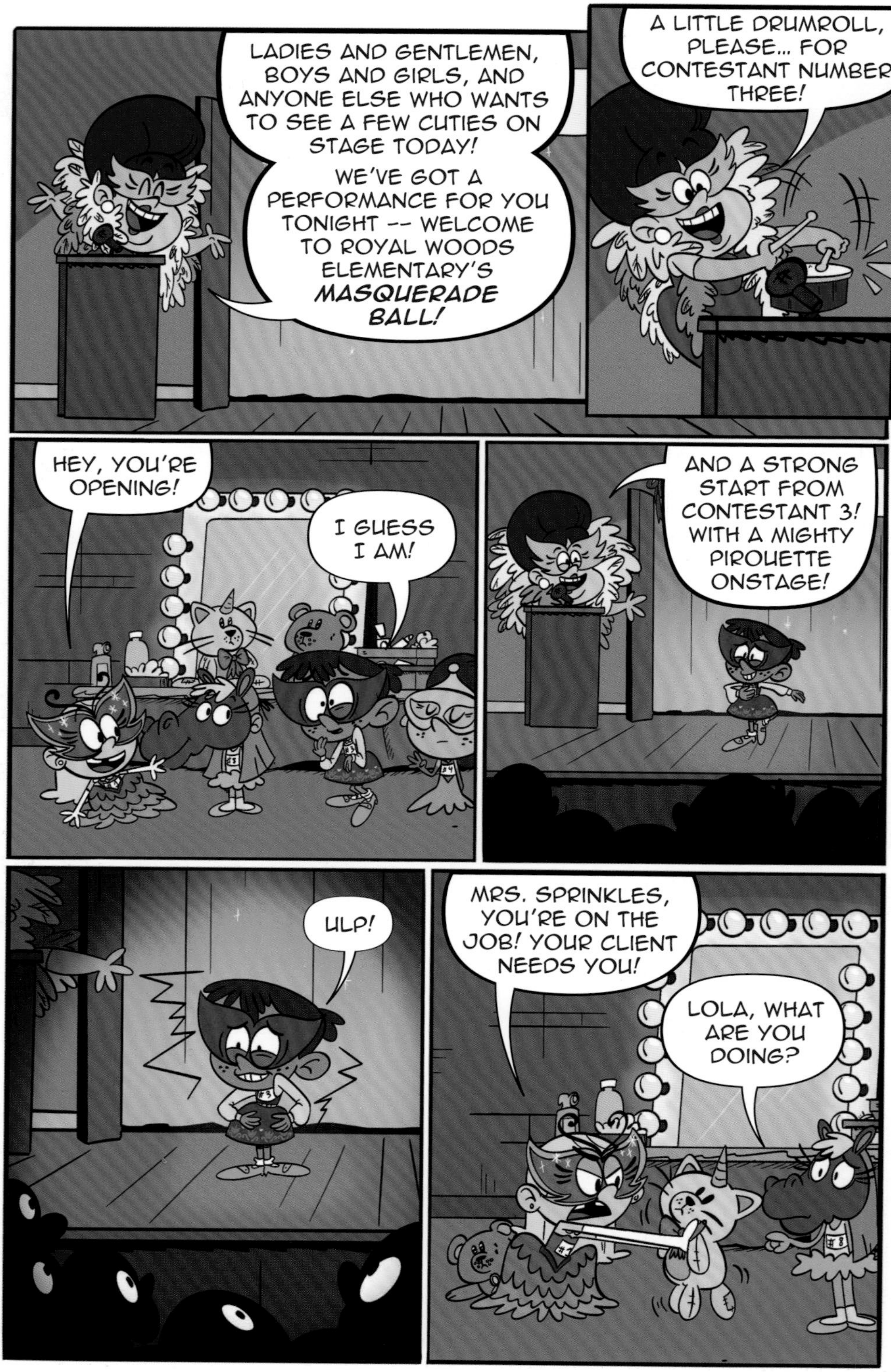
LADIES AND GENTLEMEN, BOYS AND GIRLS, AND ANYONE ELSE WHO WANTS TO SEE A FEW CUTIES ON STAGE TODAY!
WE'VE GOT A PERFORMANCE FOR YOU TONIGHT -- WELCOME TO ROYAL WOODS ELEMENTARY'S ***MASQUERADE BALL!***
A LITTLE DRUMROLL, PLEASE... FOR CONTESTANT NUMBER THREE!
HEY, YOU'RE OPENING!
I GUESS I AM!
AND A STRONG START FROM CONTESTANT 3! WITH A MIGHTY PIROUETTE ONSTAGE!
ULP!
MRS. SPRINKLES, YOU'RE ON THE JOB! YOUR CLIENT NEEDS YOU!
LOLA, WHAT ARE YOU DOING?

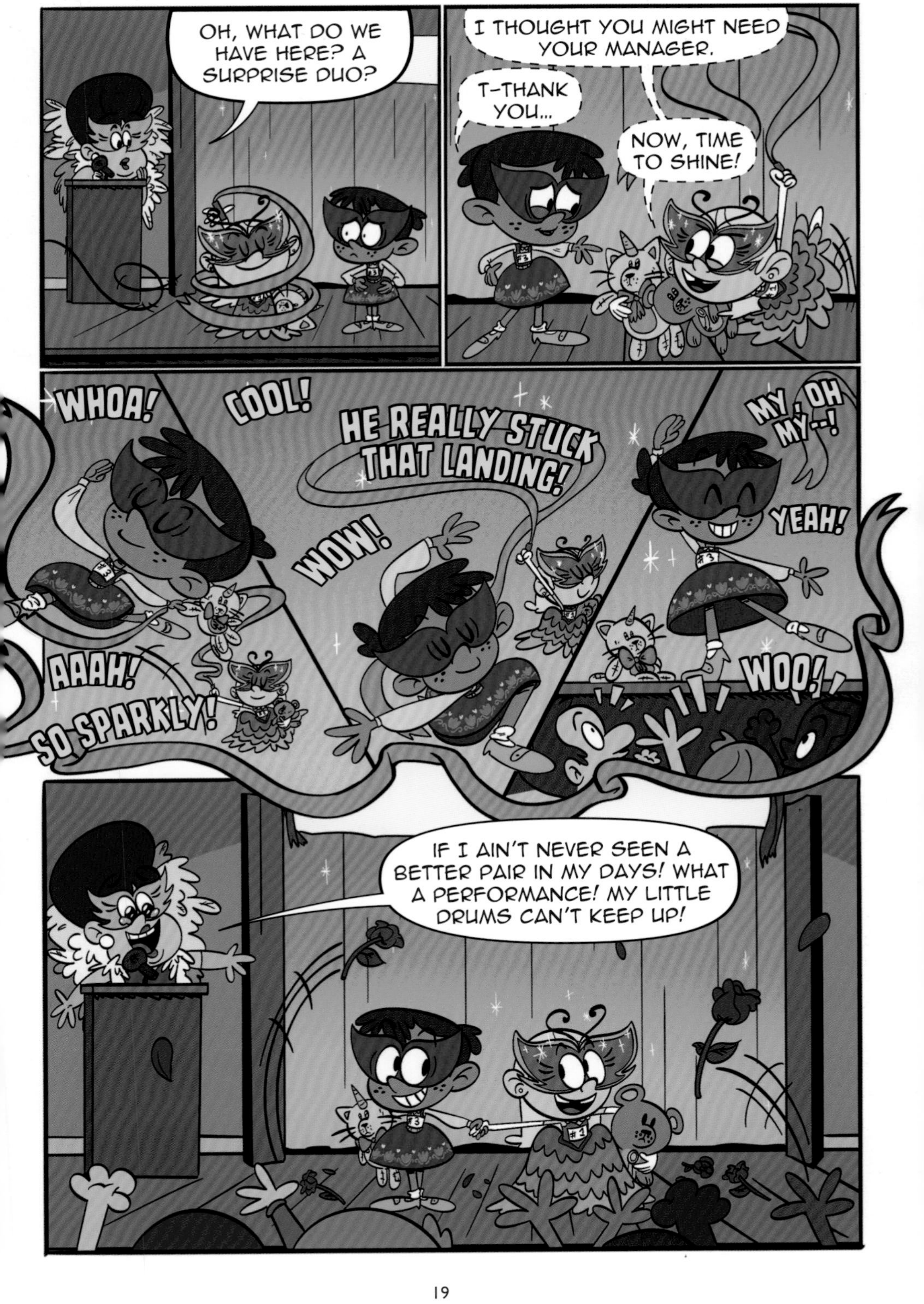
OH, WHAT DO WE HAVE HERE? A SURPRISE DUO?
I THOUGHT YOU MIGHT NEED YOUR MANAGER.
T-THANK YOU...
NOW, TIME TO SHINE!
WHOA!
COOL!
HE REALLY STUCK THAT LANDING!
MY, OH MY--!
YEAH!
WOW!
AAAH!
SO SPARKLY!
WOO!
IF I AIN'T NEVER SEEN A BETTER PAIR IN MY DAYS! WHAT A PERFORMANCE! MY LITTLE DRUMS CAN'T KEEP UP!

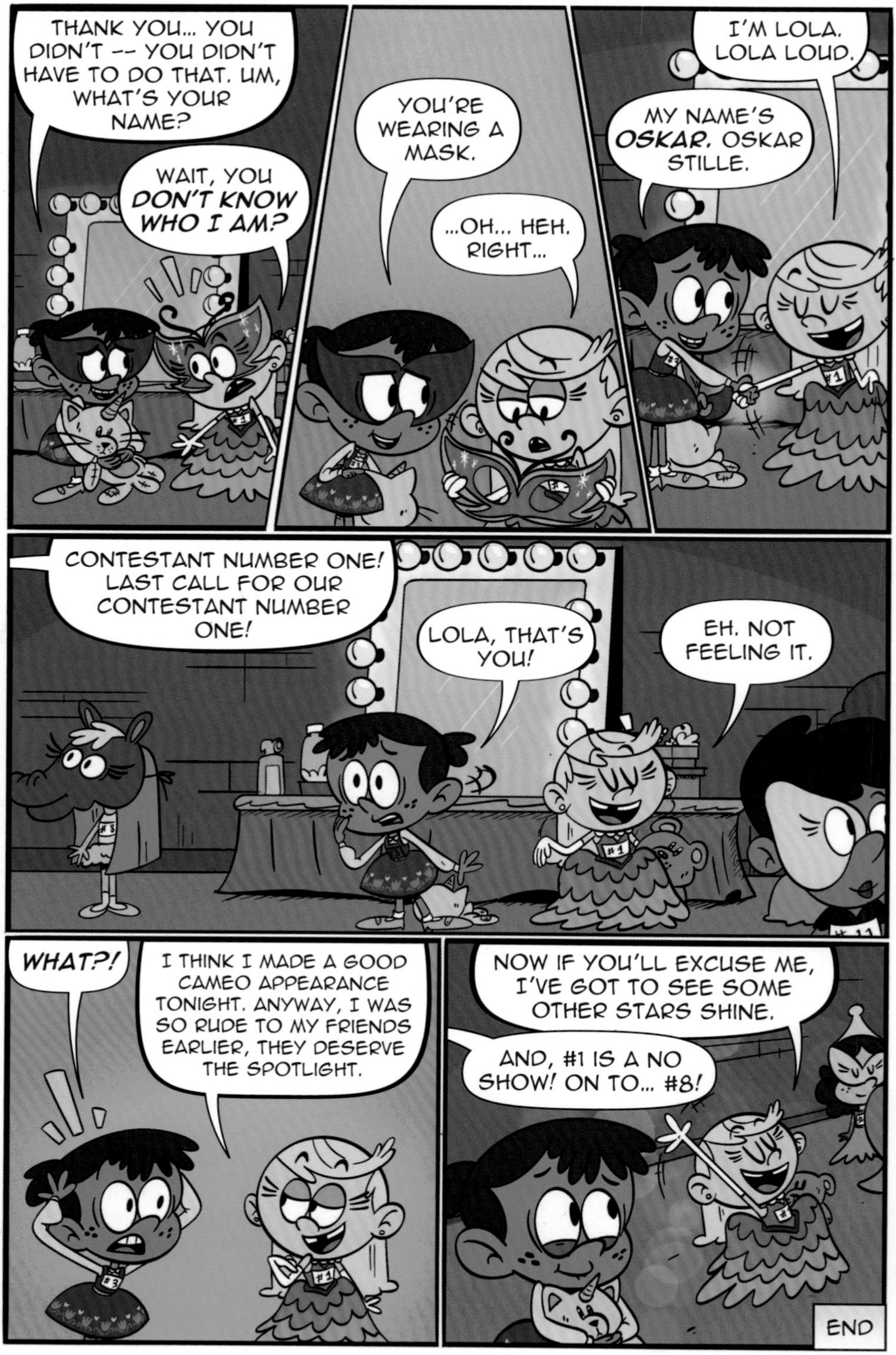
THANK YOU... YOU DIDN'T -- YOU DIDN'T HAVE TO DO THAT. UM, WHAT'S YOUR NAME?
WAIT, YOU DON'T KNOW WHO I AM?
YOU'RE WEARING A MASK.
...OH... HEH. RIGHT...
I'M LOLA. LOLA LOUD.
MY NAME'S OSKAR. OSKAR STILLE.
CONTESTANT NUMBER ONE! LAST CALL FOR OUR CONTESTANT NUMBER ONE!
LOLA, THAT'S YOU!
EH. NOT FEELING IT.
WHAT?!
I THINK I MADE A GOOD CAMEO APPEARANCE TONIGHT. ANYWAY, I WAS SO RUDE TO MY FRIENDS EARLIER, THEY DESERVE THE SPOTLIGHT.
NOW IF YOU'LL EXCUSE ME, I'VE GOT TO SEE SOME OTHER STARS SHINE.
AND, #1 IS A NO SHOW! ON TO... #8!
END

"GAME SHAME"

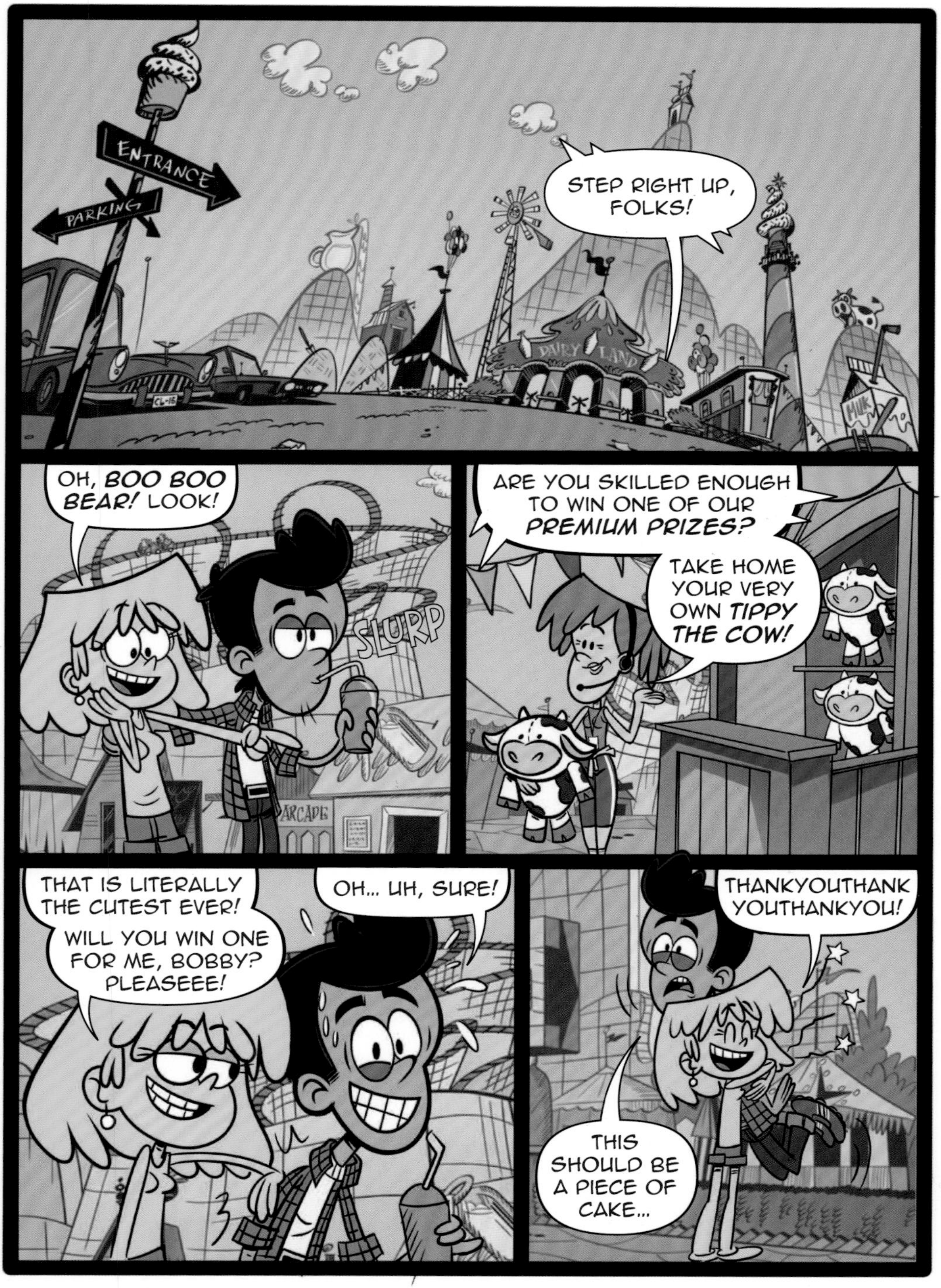
ENTRANCE
PARKING
STEP RIGHT UP, FOLKS!
DAIRY LAND
MILK
OH, BOO BOO BEAR! LOOK!
SLURP
ARCADE
ARE YOU SKILLED ENOUGH TO WIN ONE OF OUR PREMIUM PRIZES?
TAKE HOME YOUR VERY OWN TIPPY THE COW!
THAT IS LITERALLY THE CUTEST EVER!
WILL YOU WIN ONE FOR ME, BOBBY? PLEASEEE!
OH... UH, SURE!
THANKYOUTHANK YOUTHANKYOU!
THIS SHOULD BE A PIECE OF CAKE...

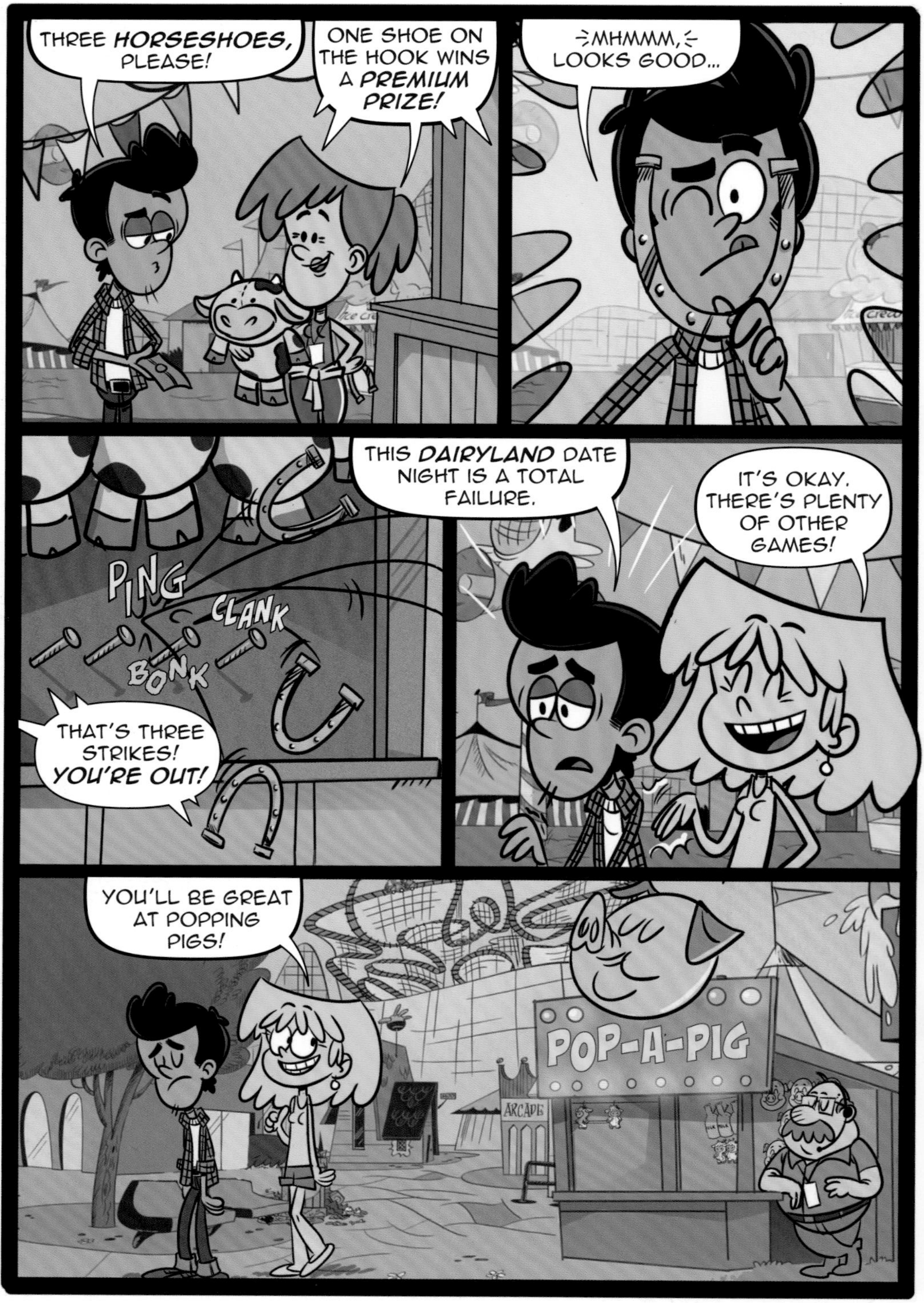
THREE *HORSESHOES,* PLEASE!
ONE SHOE ON THE HOOK WINS A ***PREMIUM PRIZE!***
MHMMM, LOOKS GOOD...
PING
CLANK
BONK
THAT'S THREE STRIKES! ***YOU'RE OUT!***
THIS ***DAIRYLAND*** DATE NIGHT IS A TOTAL FAILURE.
IT'S OKAY. THERE'S PLENTY OF OTHER GAMES!
YOU'LL BE GREAT AT POPPING PIGS!
POP-A-PIG
ARCADE

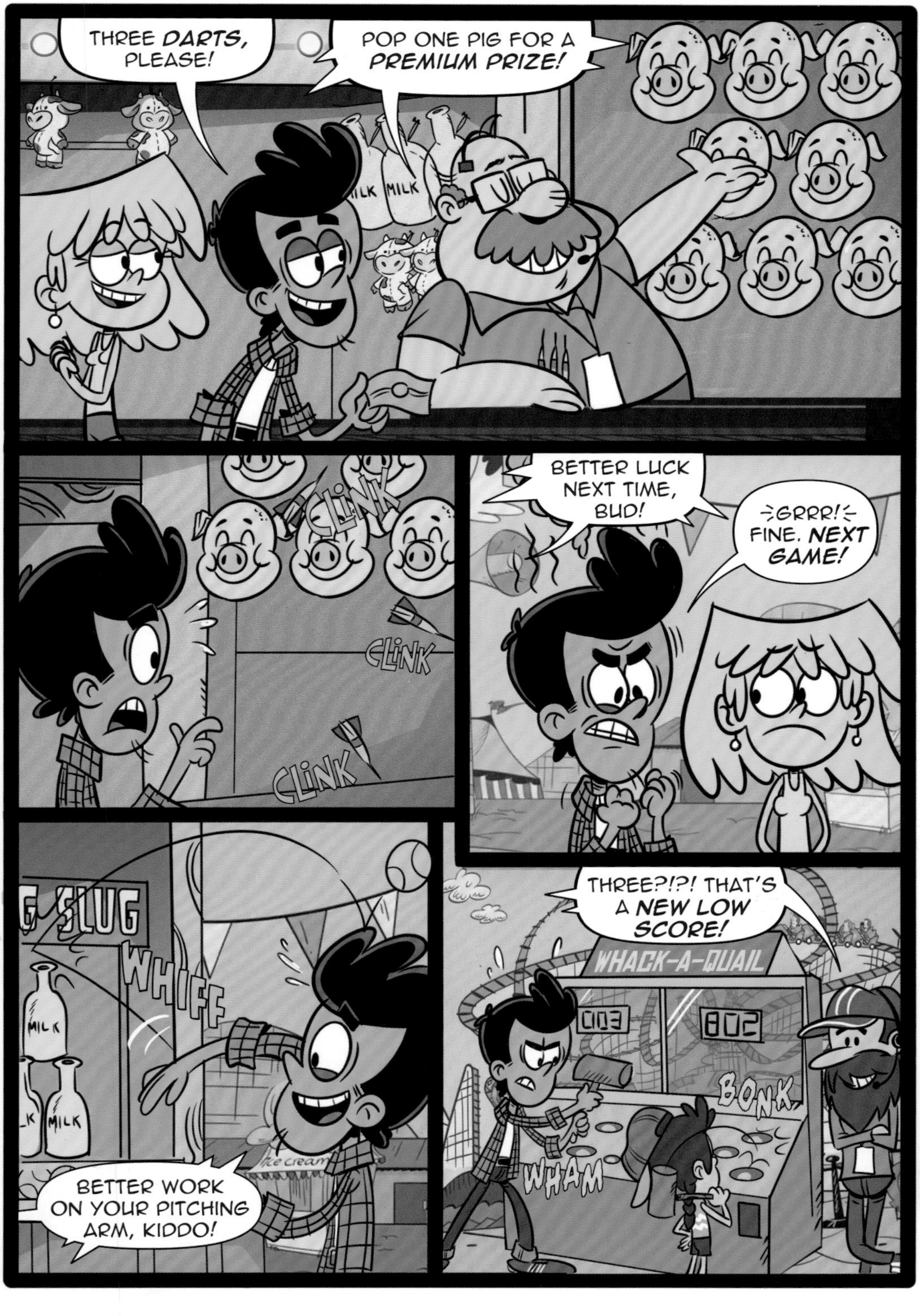

THREE DARTS, PLEASE!
POP ONE PIG FOR A PREMIUM PRIZE!
MILK
MILK
CLINK
CLINK
CLINK
BETTER LUCK NEXT TIME, BUD!
GRRR! FINE. NEXT GAME!
SLUG
WHIFF
MILK
MILK
BETTER WORK ON YOUR PITCHING ARM, KIDDO!
THREE?!?! THAT'S A NEW LOW SCORE!
WHACK-A-QUAIL
003
802
BONK
WHAM

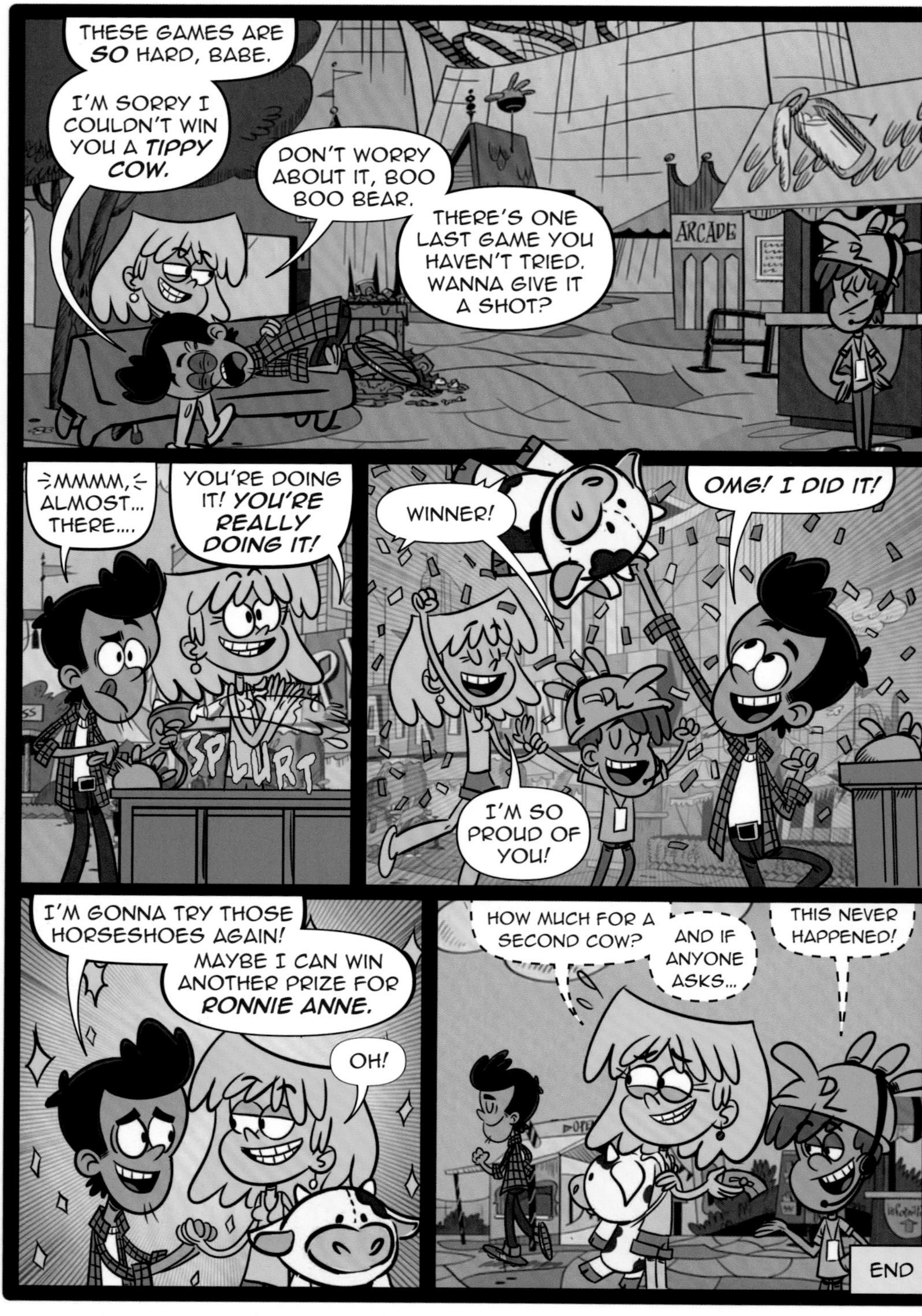
THESE GAMES ARE SO HARD, BABE.
I'M SORRY I COULDN'T WIN YOU A TIPPY COW.
DON'T WORRY ABOUT IT, BOO BOO BEAR.
THERE'S ONE LAST GAME YOU HAVEN'T TRIED. WANNA GIVE IT A SHOT?
ARCADE
MMMM, ALMOST... THERE....
YOU'RE DOING IT! YOU'RE REALLY DOING IT!
SPLURT
WINNER!
OMG! I DID IT!
I'M SO PROUD OF YOU!
I'M GONNA TRY THOSE HORSESHOES AGAIN!
MAYBE I CAN WIN ANOTHER PRIZE FOR RONNIE ANNE.
OH!
HOW MUCH FOR A SECOND COW?
AND IF ANYONE ASKS...
THIS NEVER HAPPENED!
END

"TWO LOUDS A CROWD"

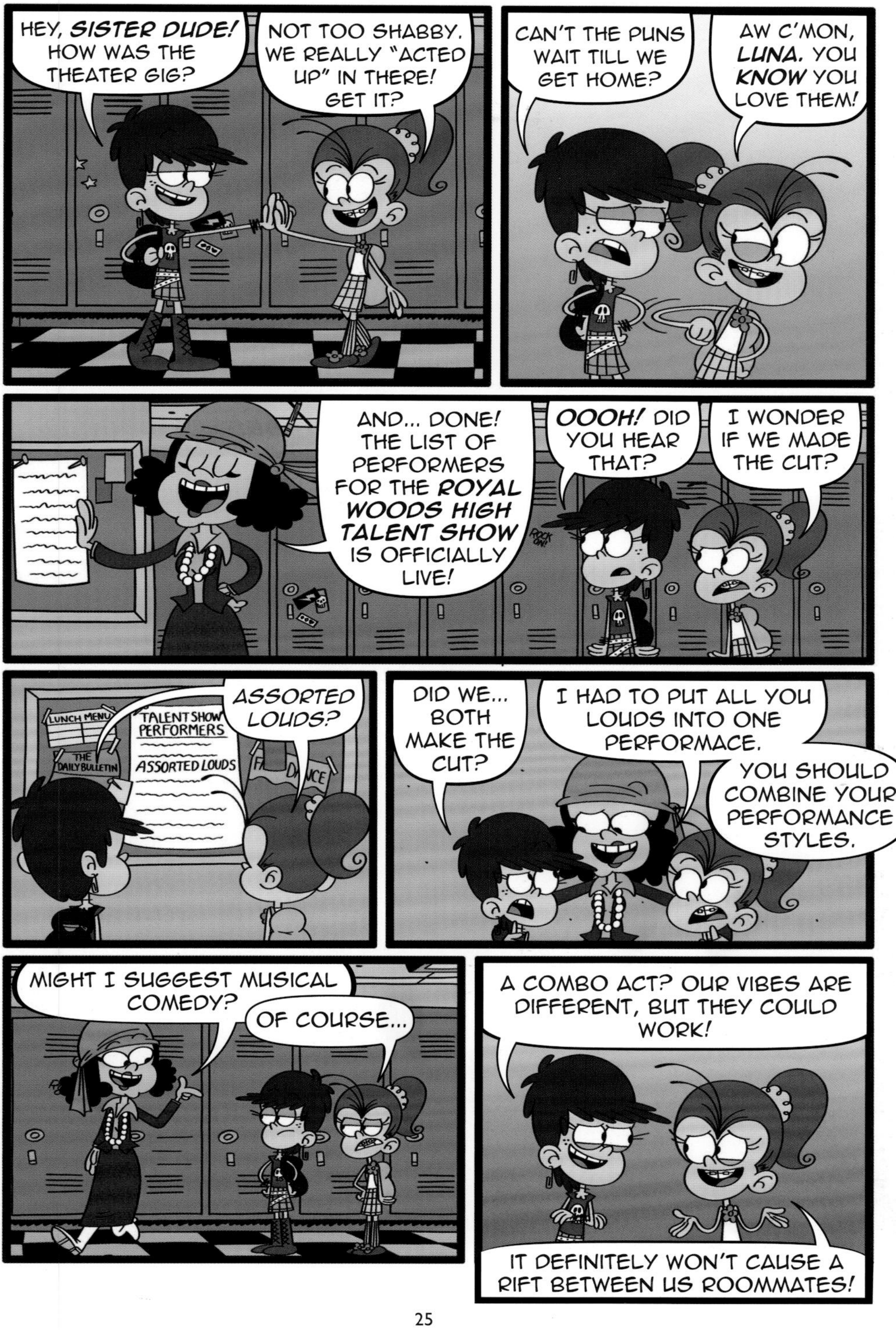
HEY, SISTER DUDE! HOW WAS THE THEATER GIG?
NOT TOO SHABBY. WE REALLY "ACTED UP" IN THERE! GET IT?
CAN'T THE PUNS WAIT TILL WE GET HOME?
AW C'MON, LUNA. YOU KNOW YOU LOVE THEM!
AND... DONE! THE LIST OF PERFORMERS FOR THE ROYAL WOODS HIGH TALENT SHOW IS OFFICIALLY LIVE!
OOOH! DID YOU HEAR THAT?
I WONDER IF WE MADE THE CUT?
ROCK ON!
LUNCH MENU
TALENT SHOW PERFORMERS
ASSORTED LOUDS
THE DAILY BULLETIN
DANCE
ASSORTED LOUDS?
DID WE... BOTH MAKE THE CUT?
I HAD TO PUT ALL YOU LOUDS INTO ONE PERFORMACE.
YOU SHOULD COMBINE YOUR PERFORMANCE STYLES.
MIGHT I SUGGEST MUSICAL COMEDY?
OF COURSE...
A COMBO ACT? OUR VIBES ARE DIFFERENT, BUT THEY COULD WORK!
IT DEFINITELY WON'T CAUSE A RIFT BETWEEN US ROOMMATES!

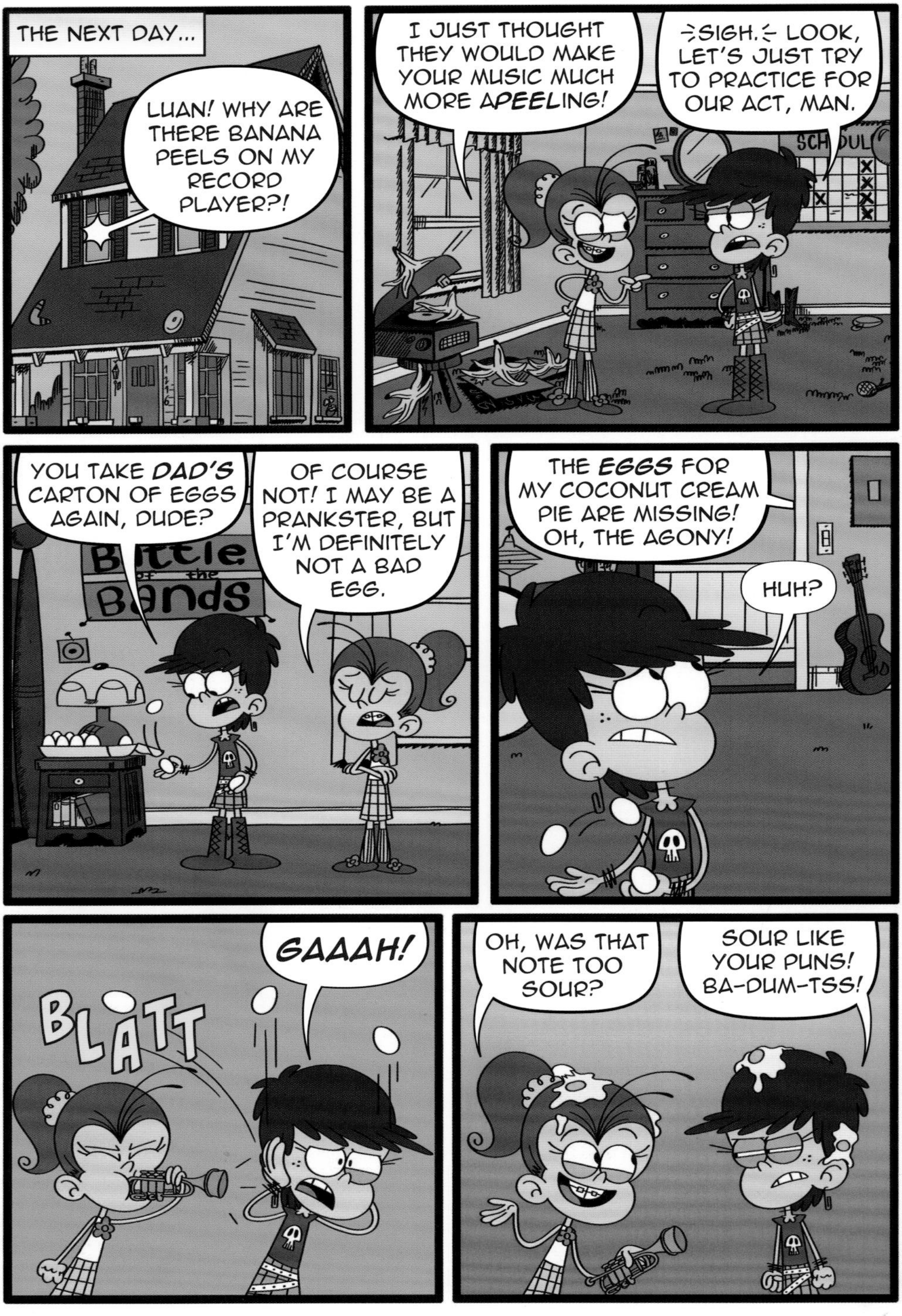

THE NEXT DAY...
LUAN! WHY ARE THERE BANANA PEELS ON MY RECORD PLAYER?!
I JUST THOUGHT THEY WOULD MAKE YOUR MUSIC MUCH MORE APEELING!
SIGH. LOOK, LET'S JUST TRY TO PRACTICE FOR OUR ACT, MAN.
SCHEDULE
YOU TAKE DAD'S CARTON OF EGGS AGAIN, DUDE?
OF COURSE NOT! I MAY BE A PRANKSTER, BUT I'M DEFINITELY NOT A BAD EGG.
Battle of the Bands
THE EGGS FOR MY COCONUT CREAM PIE ARE MISSING! OH, THE AGONY!
HUH?
GAAAH!
BLATT
OH, WAS THAT NOTE TOO SOUR?
SOUR LIKE YOUR PUNS! BA-DUM-TSS!

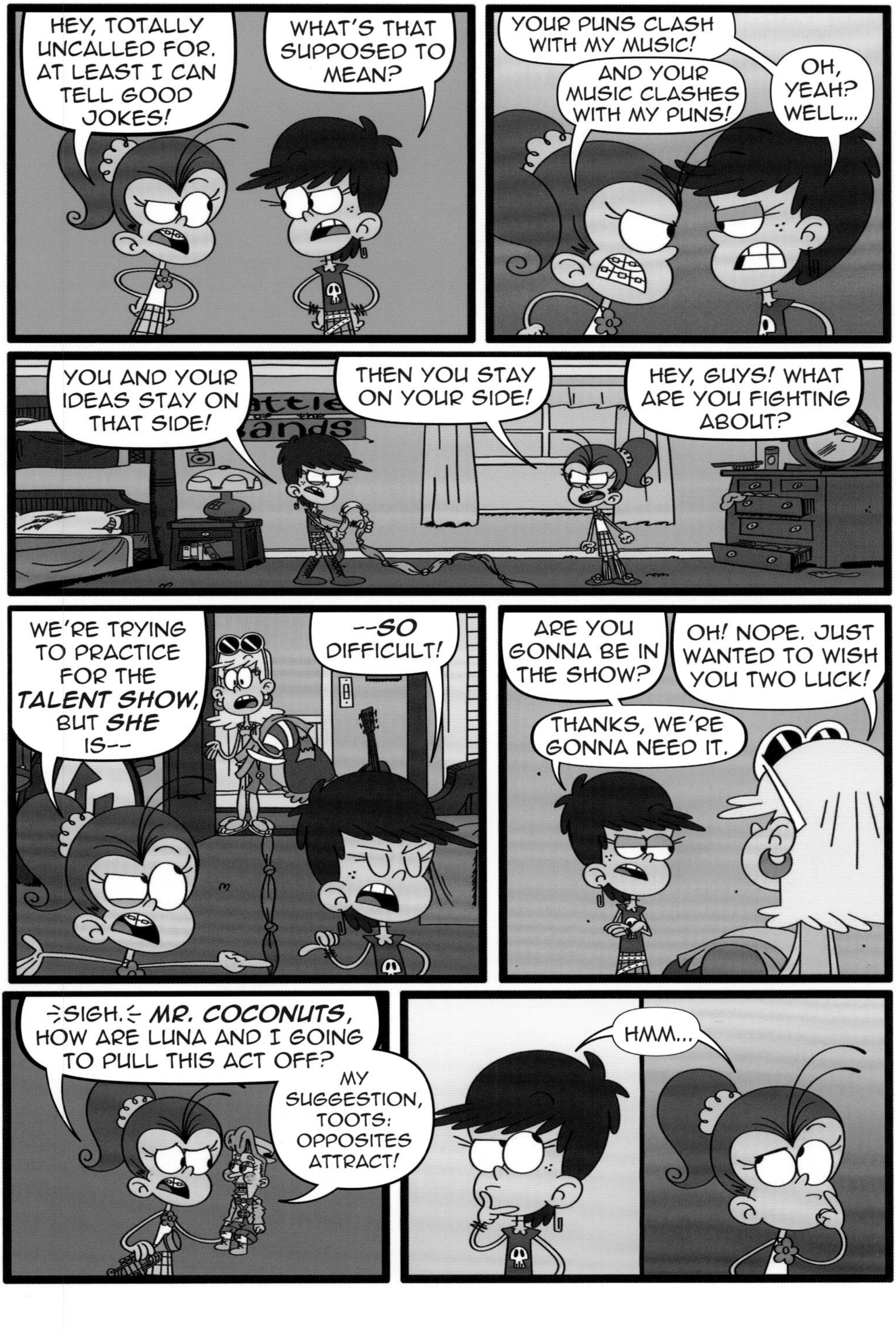
HEY, TOTALLY UNCALLED FOR. AT LEAST I CAN TELL GOOD JOKES!
WHAT'S THAT SUPPOSED TO MEAN?
YOUR PUNS CLASH WITH MY MUSIC!
AND YOUR MUSIC CLASHES WITH MY PUNS!
OH, YEAH? WELL...
YOU AND YOUR IDEAS STAY ON THAT SIDE!
THEN YOU STAY ON YOUR SIDE!
HEY, GUYS! WHAT ARE YOU FIGHTING ABOUT?
WE'RE TRYING TO PRACTICE FOR THE *TALENT SHOW*, BUT *SHE* IS--
--*SO* DIFFICULT!
ARE YOU GONNA BE IN THE SHOW?
OH! NOPE. JUST WANTED TO WISH YOU TWO LUCK!
THANKS, WE'RE GONNA NEED IT.
SIGH. *MR. COCONUTS*, HOW ARE LUNA AND I GOING TO PULL THIS ACT OFF?
MY SUGGESTION, TOOTS: OPPOSITES ATTRACT!
HMM...

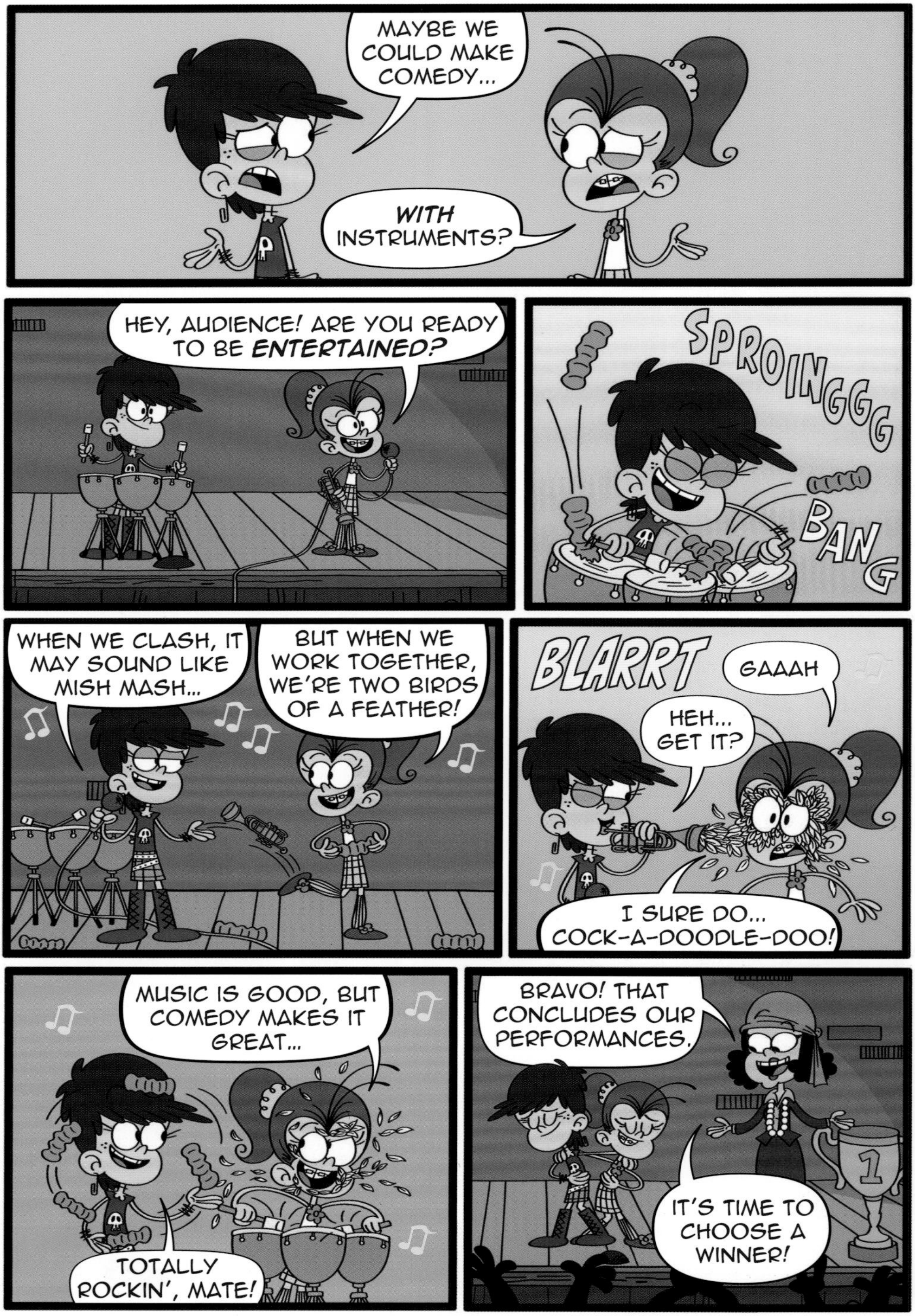
MAYBE WE COULD MAKE COMEDY...
WITH INSTRUMENTS?
HEY, AUDIENCE! ARE YOU READY TO BE ENTERTAINED?
SPROINGGG
BANG
WHEN WE CLASH, IT MAY SOUND LIKE MISH MASH...
BUT WHEN WE WORK TOGETHER, WE'RE TWO BIRDS OF A FEATHER!
BLARRT
GAAAH
HEH... GET IT?
I SURE DO... COCK-A-DOODLE-DOO!
MUSIC IS GOOD, BUT COMEDY MAKES IT GREAT...
TOTALLY ROCKIN', MATE!
BRAVO! THAT CONCLUDES OUR PERFORMANCES.
IT'S TIME TO CHOOSE A WINNER!

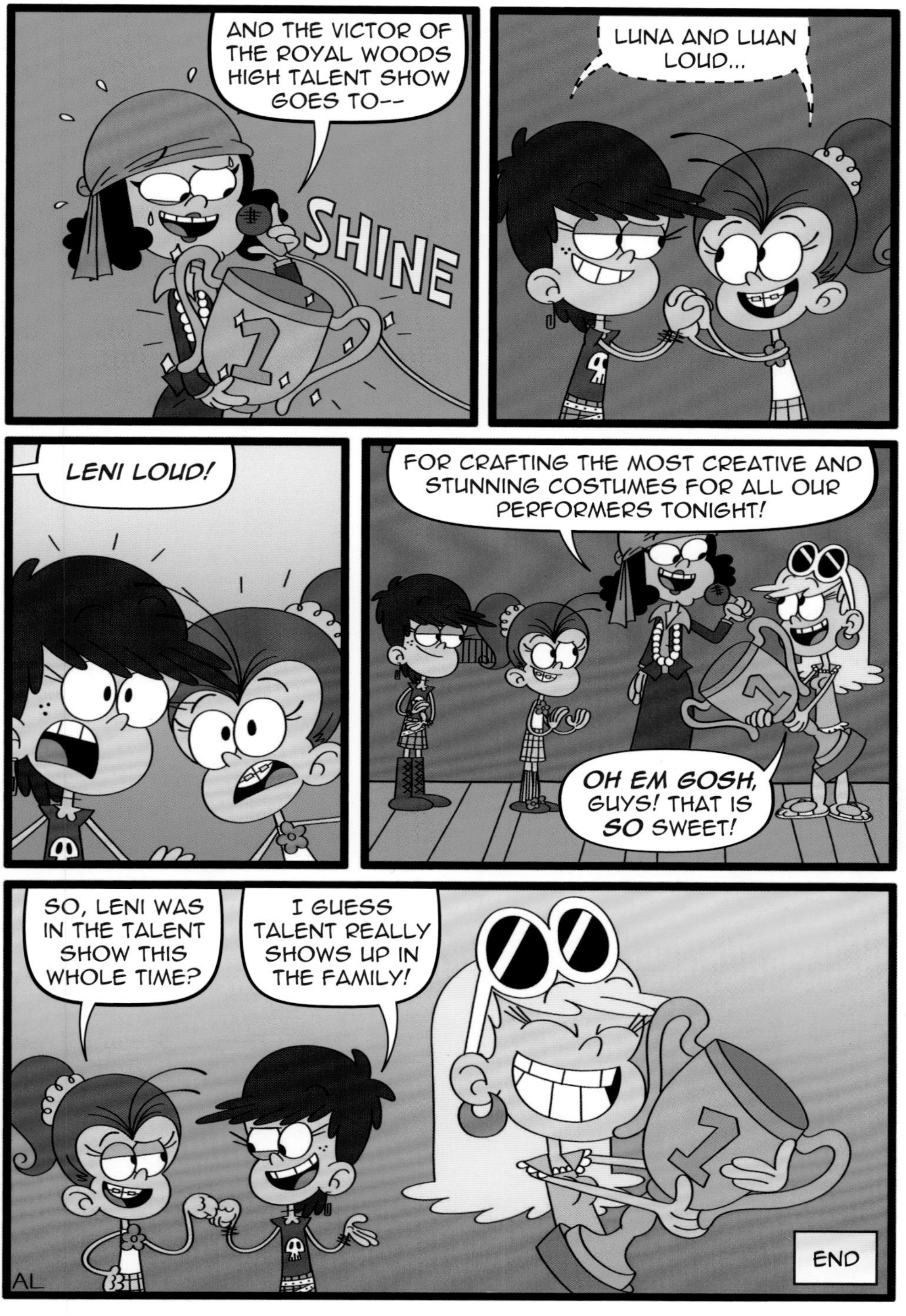
AND THE VICTOR OF THE ROYAL WOODS HIGH TALENT SHOW GOES TO--
SHINE
LUNA AND LUAN LOUD...
LENI LOUD!
FOR CRAFTING THE MOST CREATIVE AND STUNNING COSTUMES FOR ALL OUR PERFORMERS TONIGHT!
OH EM GOSH, GUYS! THAT IS SO SWEET!
SO, LENI WAS IN THE TALENT SHOW THIS WHOLE TIME?
I GUESS TALENT REALLY SHOWS UP IN THE FAMILY!
END
AL

"THE PERFECT CHEESE"

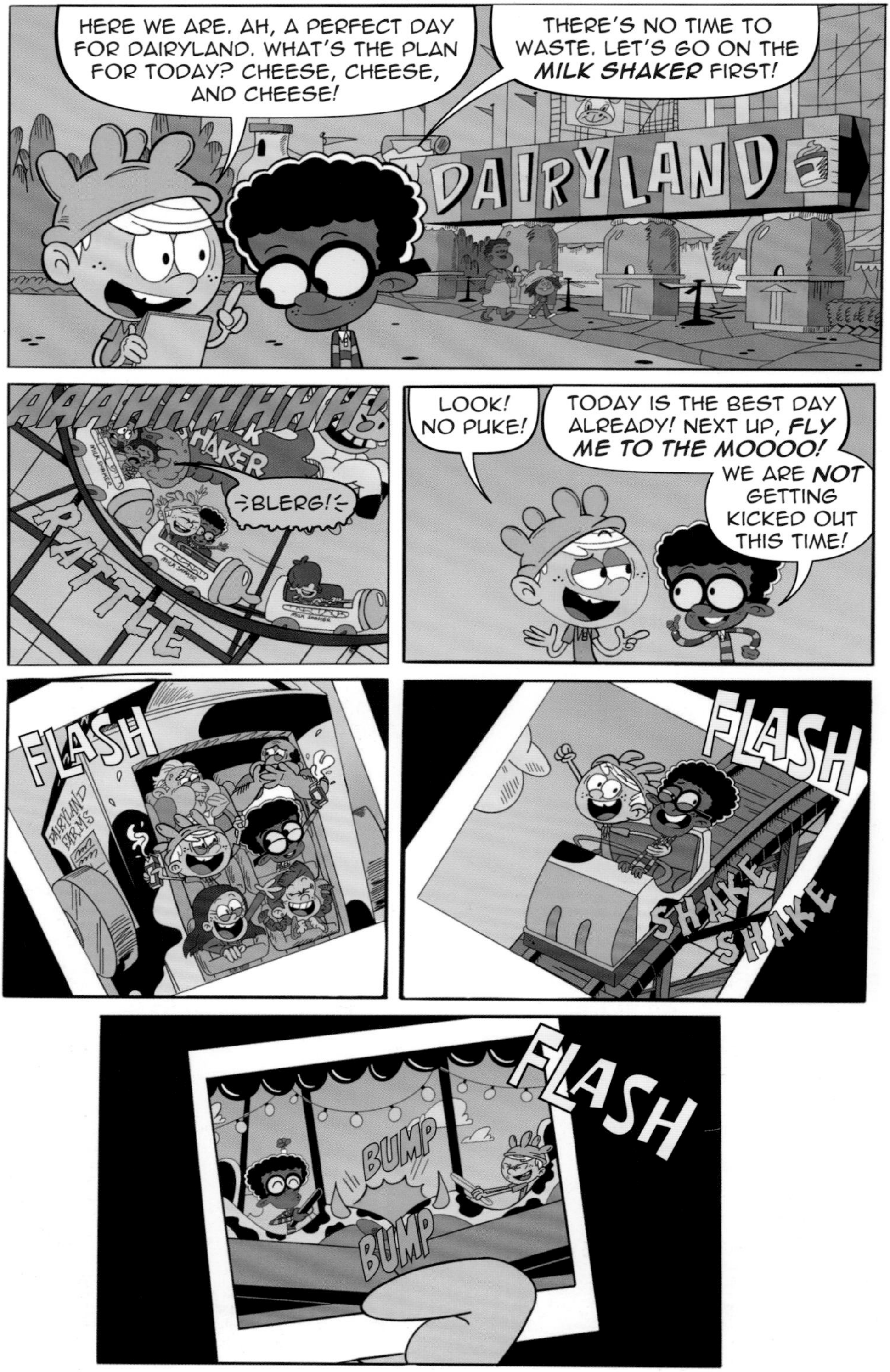
HERE WE ARE. AH, A PERFECT DAY FOR DAIRYLAND. WHAT'S THE PLAN FOR TODAY? CHEESE, CHEESE, AND CHEESE!
THERE'S NO TIME TO WASTE. LET'S GO ON THE MILK SHAKER FIRST!
DAIRYLAND
AAAHHHHHHH!
SHAKER
BLERG!
RATTLE
LOOK! NO PUKE!
TODAY IS THE BEST DAY ALREADY! NEXT UP, FLY ME TO THE MOOOO!
WE ARE NOT GETTING KICKED OUT THIS TIME!
FLASH
DAIRYLAND FARMS
FLASH
SHAKE
SHAKE
FLASH
BUMP
BUMP

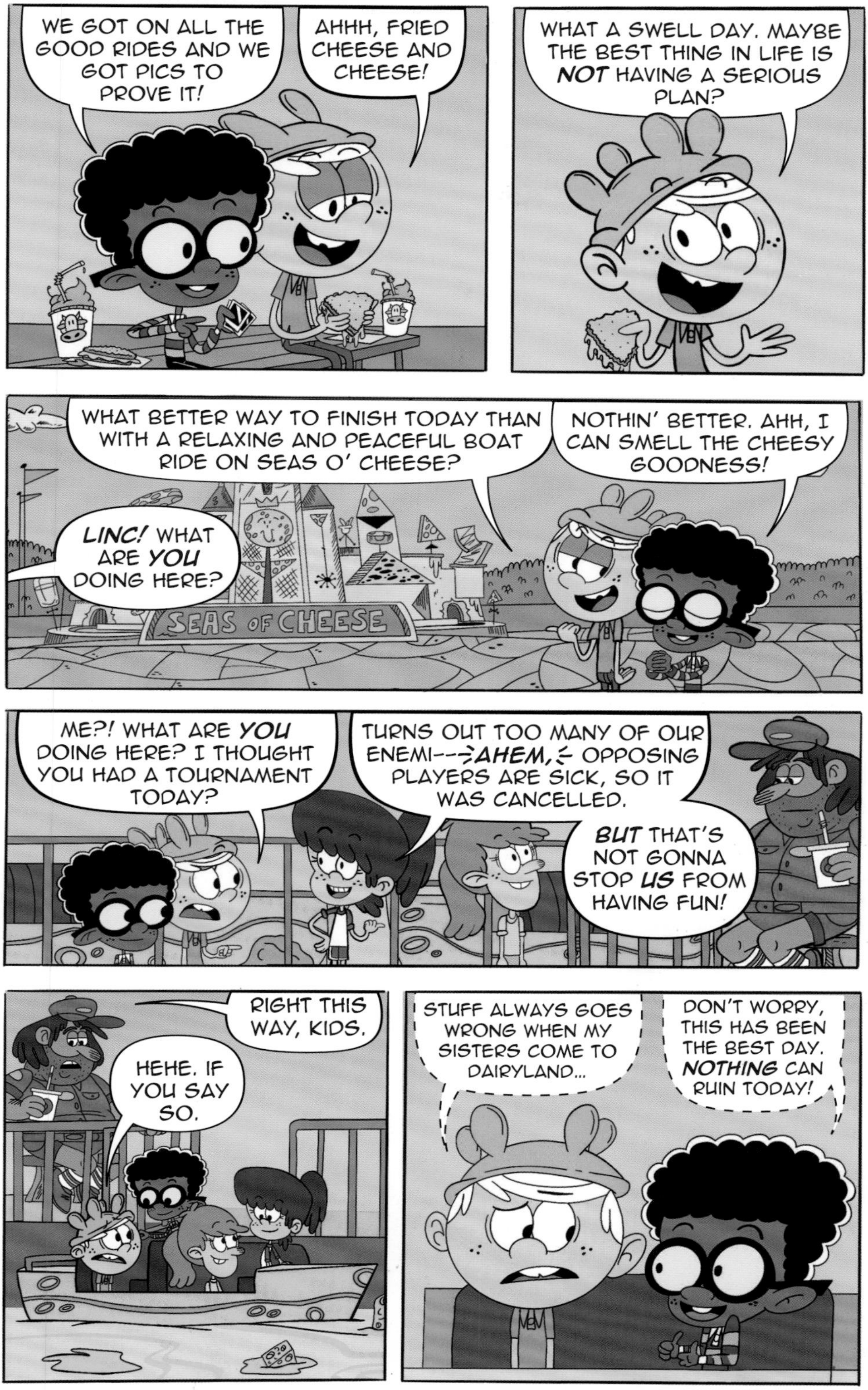
WE GOT ON ALL THE GOOD RIDES AND WE GOT PICS TO PROVE IT!
AHHH, FRIED CHEESE AND CHEESE!
WHAT A SWELL DAY. MAYBE THE BEST THING IN LIFE IS NOT HAVING A SERIOUS PLAN?
WHAT BETTER WAY TO FINISH TODAY THAN WITH A RELAXING AND PEACEFUL BOAT RIDE ON SEAS O' CHEESE?
NOTHIN' BETTER. AHH, I CAN SMELL THE CHEESY GOODNESS!
LINC! WHAT ARE YOU DOING HERE?
SEAS OF CHEESE
ME?! WHAT ARE YOU DOING HERE? I THOUGHT YOU HAD A TOURNAMENT TODAY?
TURNS OUT TOO MANY OF OUR ENEMI-- AHEM, OPPOSING PLAYERS ARE SICK, SO IT WAS CANCELLED.
BUT THAT'S NOT GONNA STOP US FROM HAVING FUN!
RIGHT THIS WAY, KIDS.
HEHE. IF YOU SAY SO.
STUFF ALWAYS GOES WRONG WHEN MY SISTERS COME TO DAIRYLAND...
DON'T WORRY, THIS HAS BEEN THE BEST DAY. NOTHING CAN RUIN TODAY!

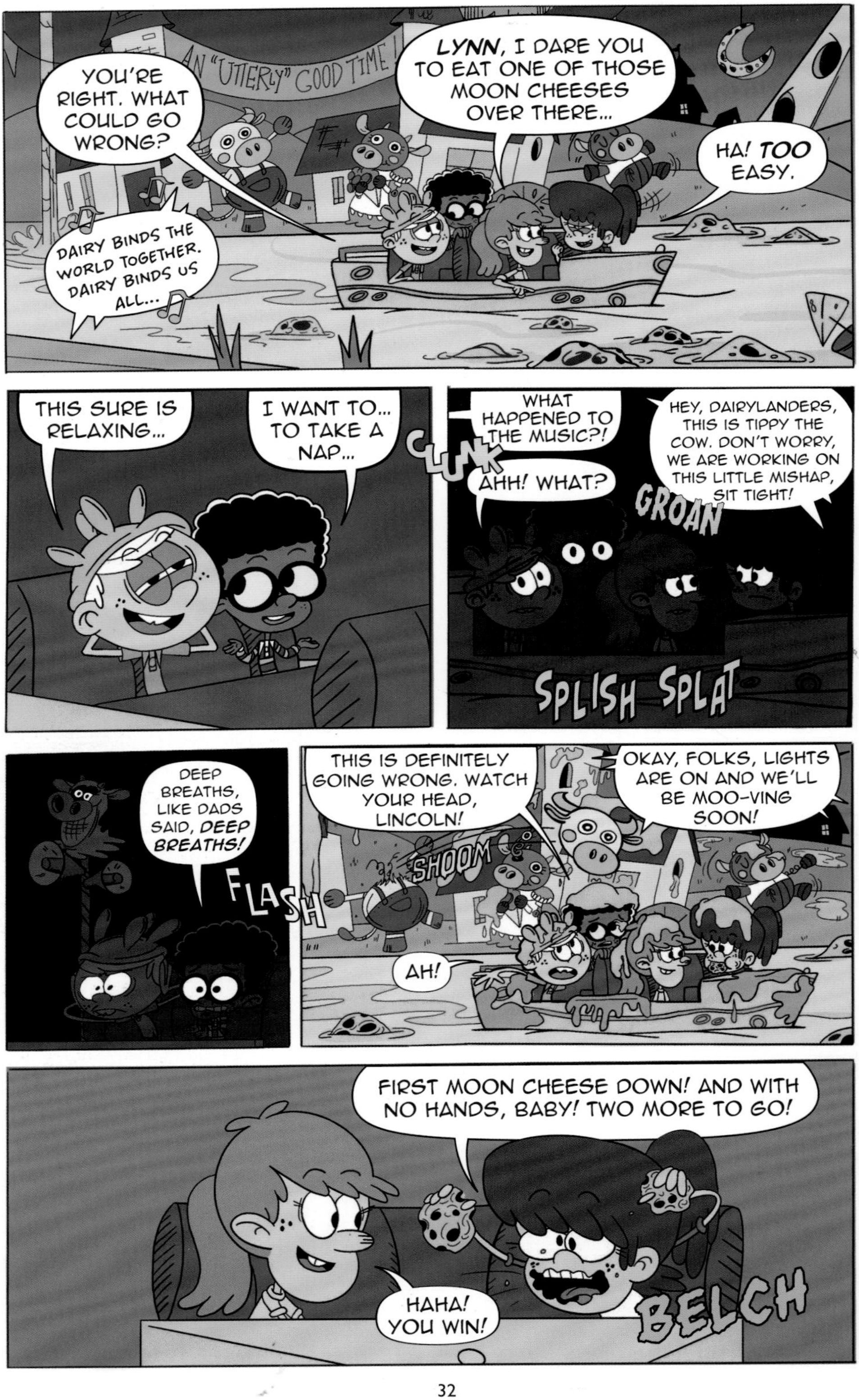
AN "UTTERLY" GOOD TIME!
YOU'RE RIGHT. WHAT COULD GO WRONG?
LYNN, I DARE YOU TO EAT ONE OF THOSE MOON CHEESES OVER THERE...
HA! TOO EASY.
DAIRY BINDS THE WORLD TOGETHER. DAIRY BINDS US ALL...
THIS SURE IS RELAXING...
I WANT TO... TO TAKE A NAP...
CLUNK
WHAT HAPPENED TO THE MUSIC?!
AHH! WHAT?
HEY, DAIRYLANDERS, THIS IS TIPPY THE COW. DON'T WORRY, WE ARE WORKING ON THIS LITTLE MISHAP, SIT TIGHT!
GROAN
SPLISH SPLAT
DEEP BREATHS, LIKE DADS SAID, DEEP BREATHS!
FLASH
THIS IS DEFINITELY GOING WRONG. WATCH YOUR HEAD, LINCOLN!
OKAY, FOLKS, LIGHTS ARE ON AND WE'LL BE MOO-VING SOON!
SHOOM
AH!
FIRST MOON CHEESE DOWN! AND WITH NO HANDS, BABY! TWO MORE TO GO!
HAHA! YOU WIN!
BELCH

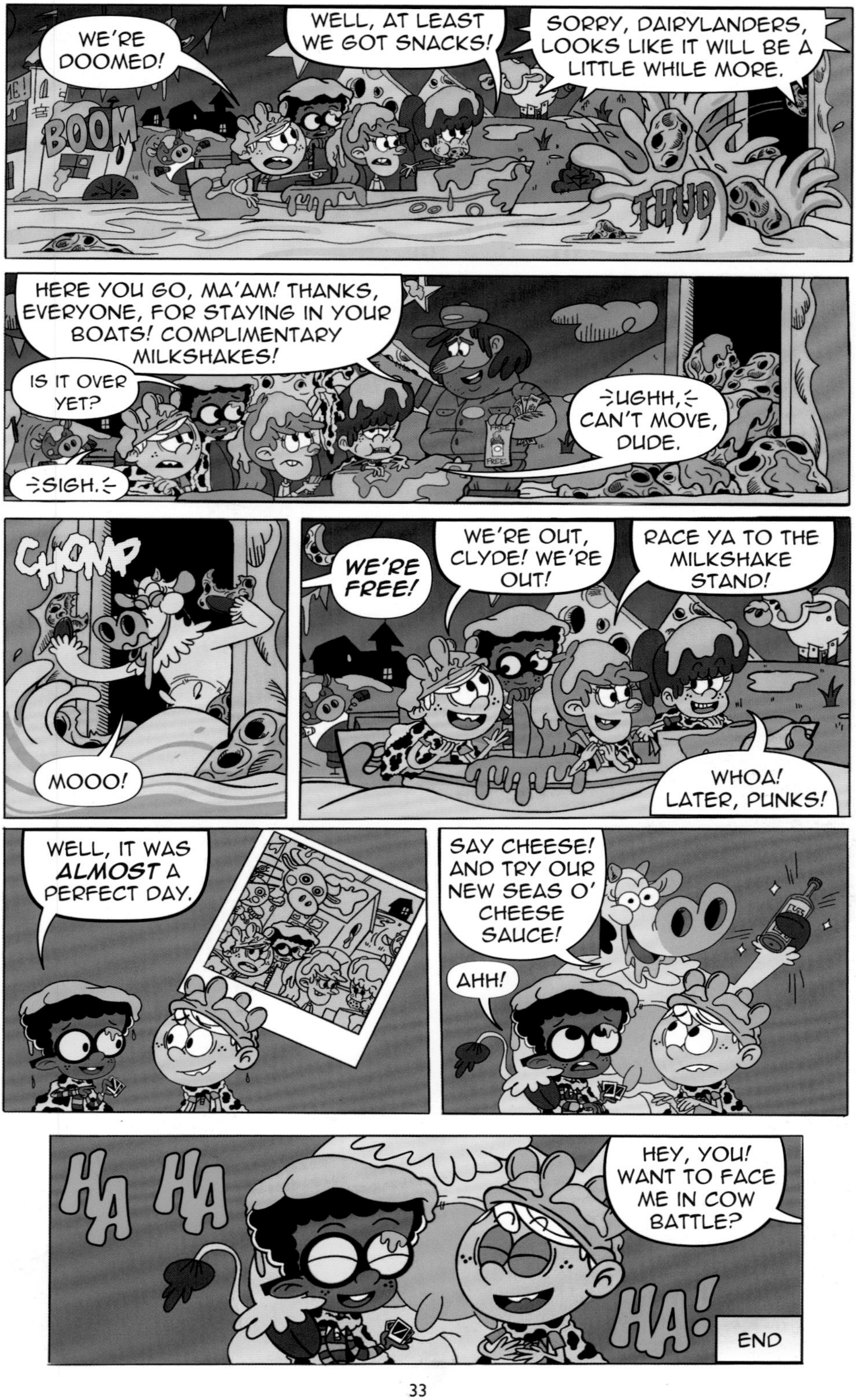
WE'RE DOOMED!
WELL, AT LEAST WE GOT SNACKS!
SORRY, DAIRYLANDERS, LOOKS LIKE IT WILL BE A LITTLE WHILE MORE.
BOOM
THUD
HERE YOU GO, MA'AM! THANKS, EVERYONE, FOR STAYING IN YOUR BOATS! COMPLIMENTARY MILKSHAKES!
IS IT OVER YET?
SIGH.
UGHH, CAN'T MOVE, DUDE.
CHOMP
MOOO!
WE'RE FREE!
WE'RE OUT, CLYDE! WE'RE OUT!
RACE YA TO THE MILKSHAKE STAND!
WHOA! LATER, PUNKS!
WELL, IT WAS ALMOST A PERFECT DAY.
SAY CHEESE! AND TRY OUR NEW SEAS O' CHEESE SAUCE!
AHH!
HA HA
HEY, YOU! WANT TO FACE ME IN COW BATTLE?
HA!
END

"NIGHT WALKER"

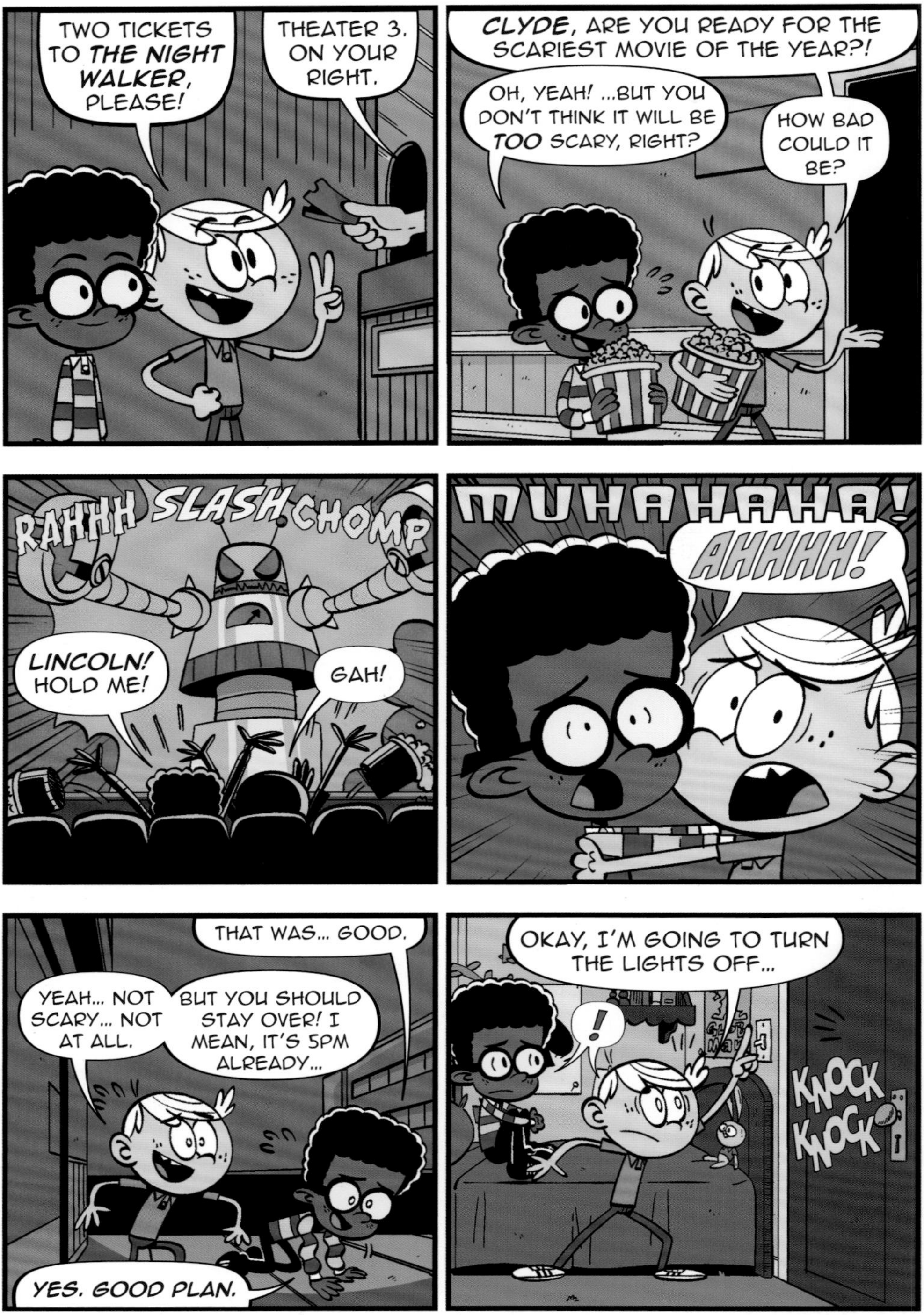
TWO TICKETS TO THE NIGHT WALKER, PLEASE!
THEATER 3. ON YOUR RIGHT.
CLYDE, ARE YOU READY FOR THE SCARIEST MOVIE OF THE YEAR?!
OH, YEAH! ...BUT YOU DON'T THINK IT WILL BE TOO SCARY, RIGHT?
HOW BAD COULD IT BE?
RAHHH SLASH CHOMP
LINCOLN! HOLD ME!
GAH!
MUHAHAHAHA!
AHHHH!
THAT WAS... GOOD.
YEAH... NOT SCARY... NOT AT ALL.
BUT YOU SHOULD STAY OVER! I MEAN, IT'S 5PM ALREADY...
YES. GOOD PLAN.
OKAY, I'M GOING TO TURN THE LIGHTS OFF...
!
KNOCK KNOCK

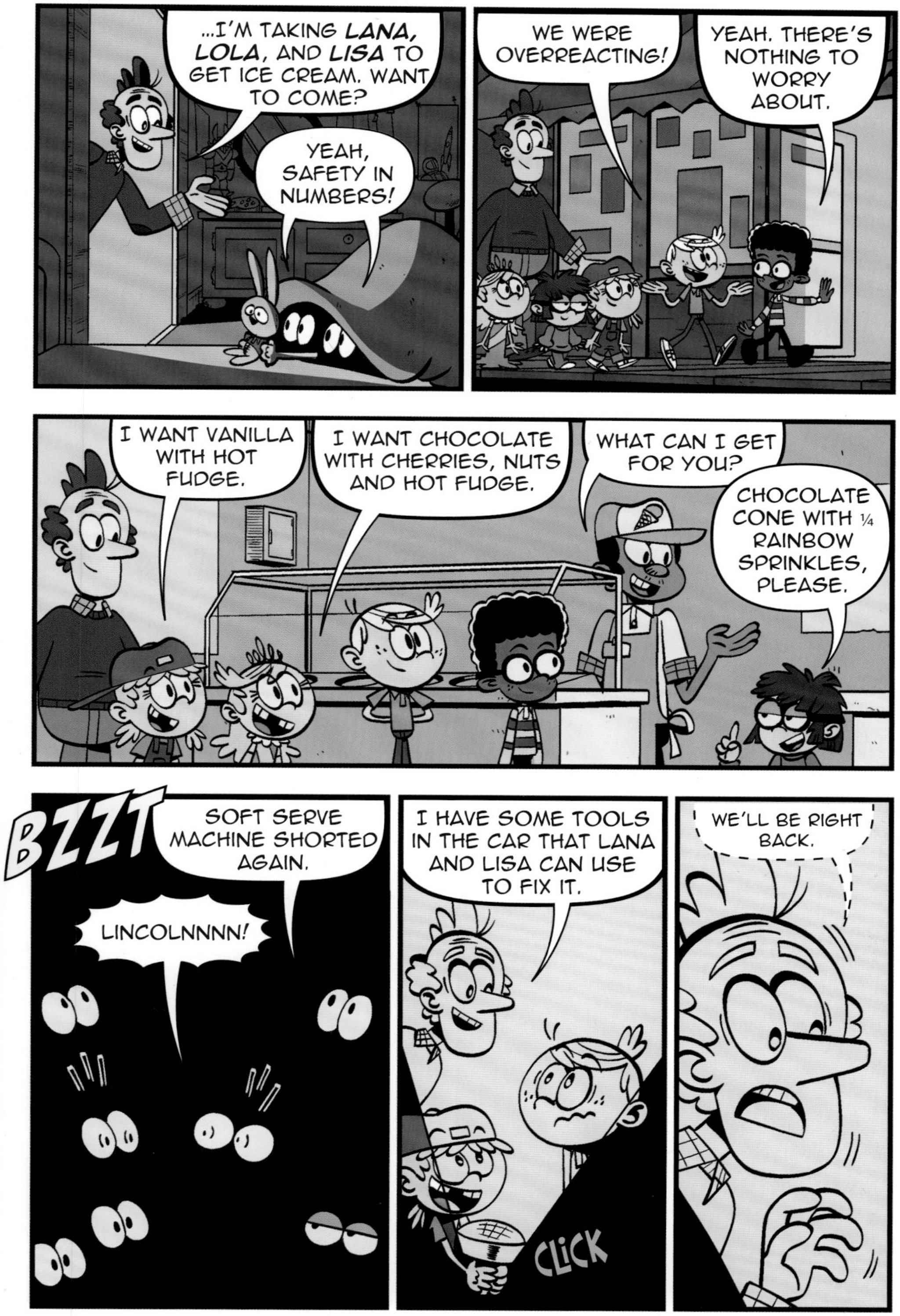

...I'M TAKING LANA, LOLA, AND LISA TO GET ICE CREAM. WANT TO COME?
YEAH, SAFETY IN NUMBERS!
WE WERE OVERREACTING!
YEAH. THERE'S NOTHING TO WORRY ABOUT.
I WANT VANILLA WITH HOT FUDGE.
I WANT CHOCOLATE WITH CHERRIES, NUTS AND HOT FUDGE.
WHAT CAN I GET FOR YOU?
CHOCOLATE CONE WITH ¼ RAINBOW SPRINKLES, PLEASE.
BZZT
SOFT SERVE MACHINE SHORTED AGAIN.
LINCOLNNNN!
I HAVE SOME TOOLS IN THE CAR THAT LANA AND LISA CAN USE TO FIX IT.
CLICK
WE'LL BE RIGHT BACK.

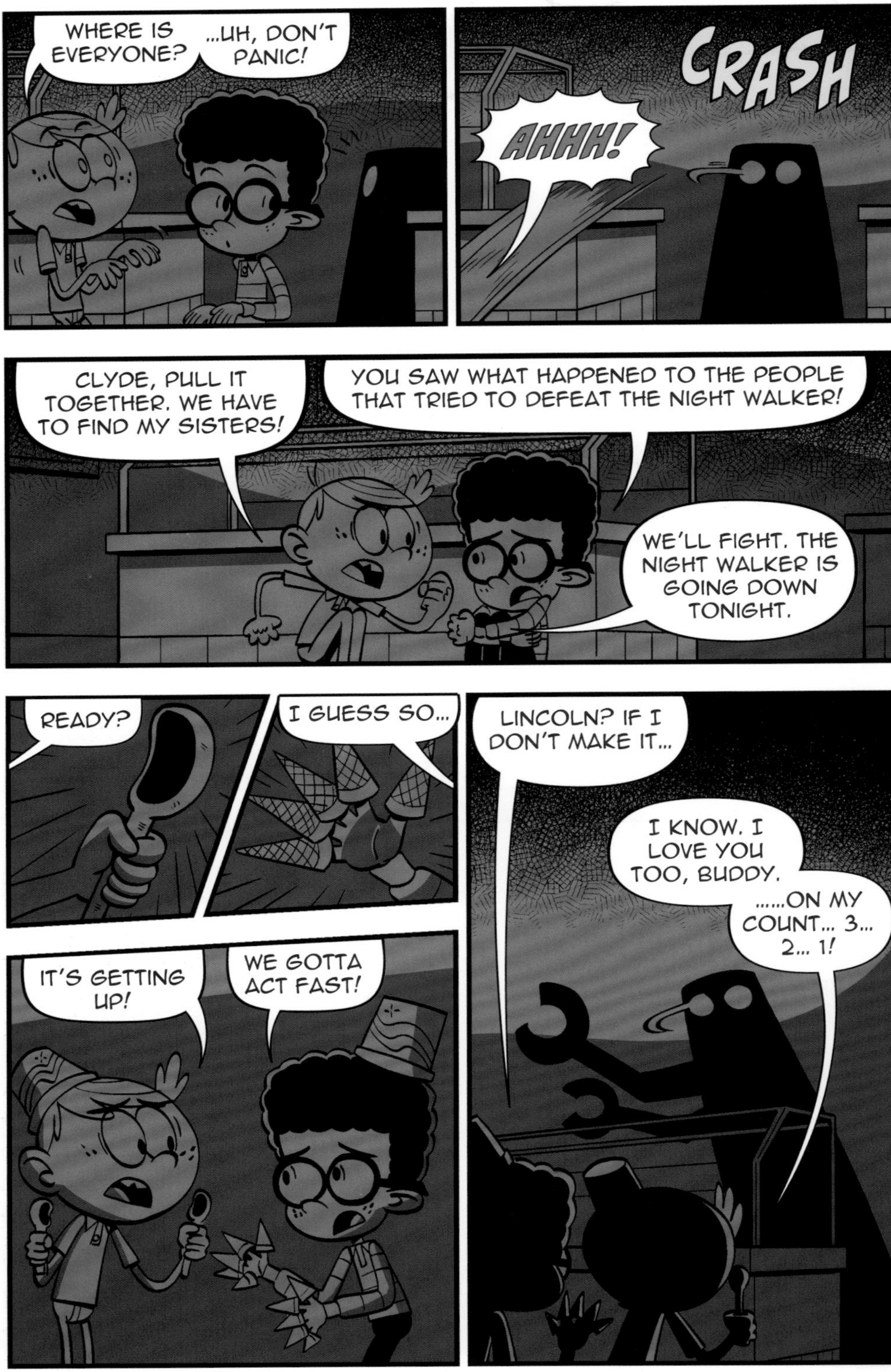

WHERE IS EVERYONE?
...UH, DON'T PANIC!
CRASH
AHHH!
CLYDE, PULL IT TOGETHER. WE HAVE TO FIND MY SISTERS!
YOU SAW WHAT HAPPENED TO THE PEOPLE THAT TRIED TO DEFEAT THE NIGHT WALKER!
WE'LL FIGHT. THE NIGHT WALKER IS GOING DOWN TONIGHT.
READY?
I GUESS SO...
IT'S GETTING UP!
WE GOTTA ACT FAST!
LINCOLN? IF I DON'T MAKE IT...
I KNOW. I LOVE YOU TOO, BUDDY.
......ON MY COUNT... 3... 2... 1!

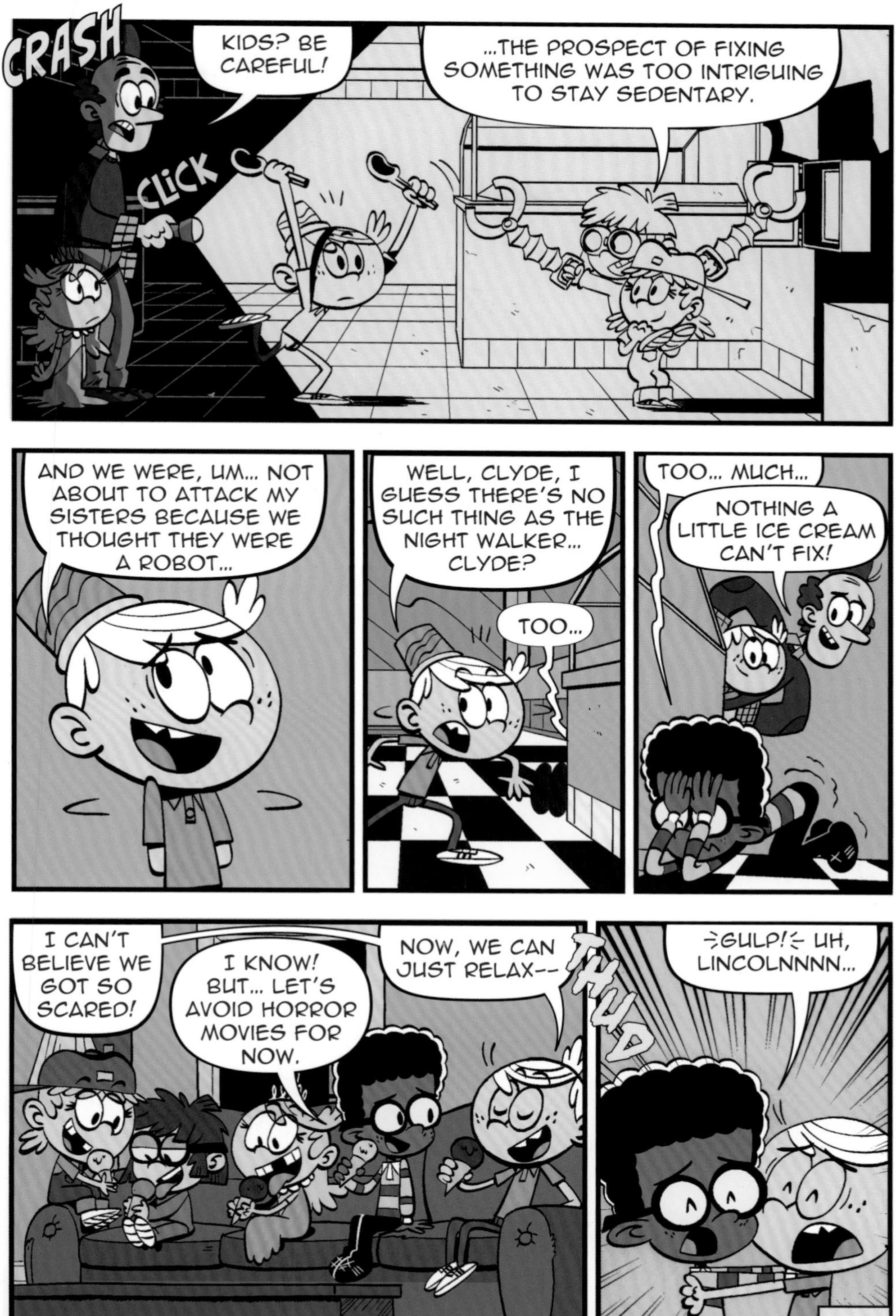

CRASH
KIDS? BE CAREFUL!
CLICK
...THE PROSPECT OF FIXING SOMETHING WAS TOO INTRIGUING TO STAY SEDENTARY.
AND WE WERE, UM... NOT ABOUT TO ATTACK MY SISTERS BECAUSE WE THOUGHT THEY WERE A ROBOT...
WELL, CLYDE, I GUESS THERE'S NO SUCH THING AS THE NIGHT WALKER... CLYDE?
TOO...
TOO... MUCH...
NOTHING A LITTLE ICE CREAM CAN'T FIX!
I CAN'T BELIEVE WE GOT SO SCARED!
I KNOW! BUT... LET'S AVOID HORROR MOVIES FOR NOW.
NOW, WE CAN JUST RELAX--
THUD
GULP! UH, LINCOLNNNN...
END

"NOTHING BUT THE TOOTH"

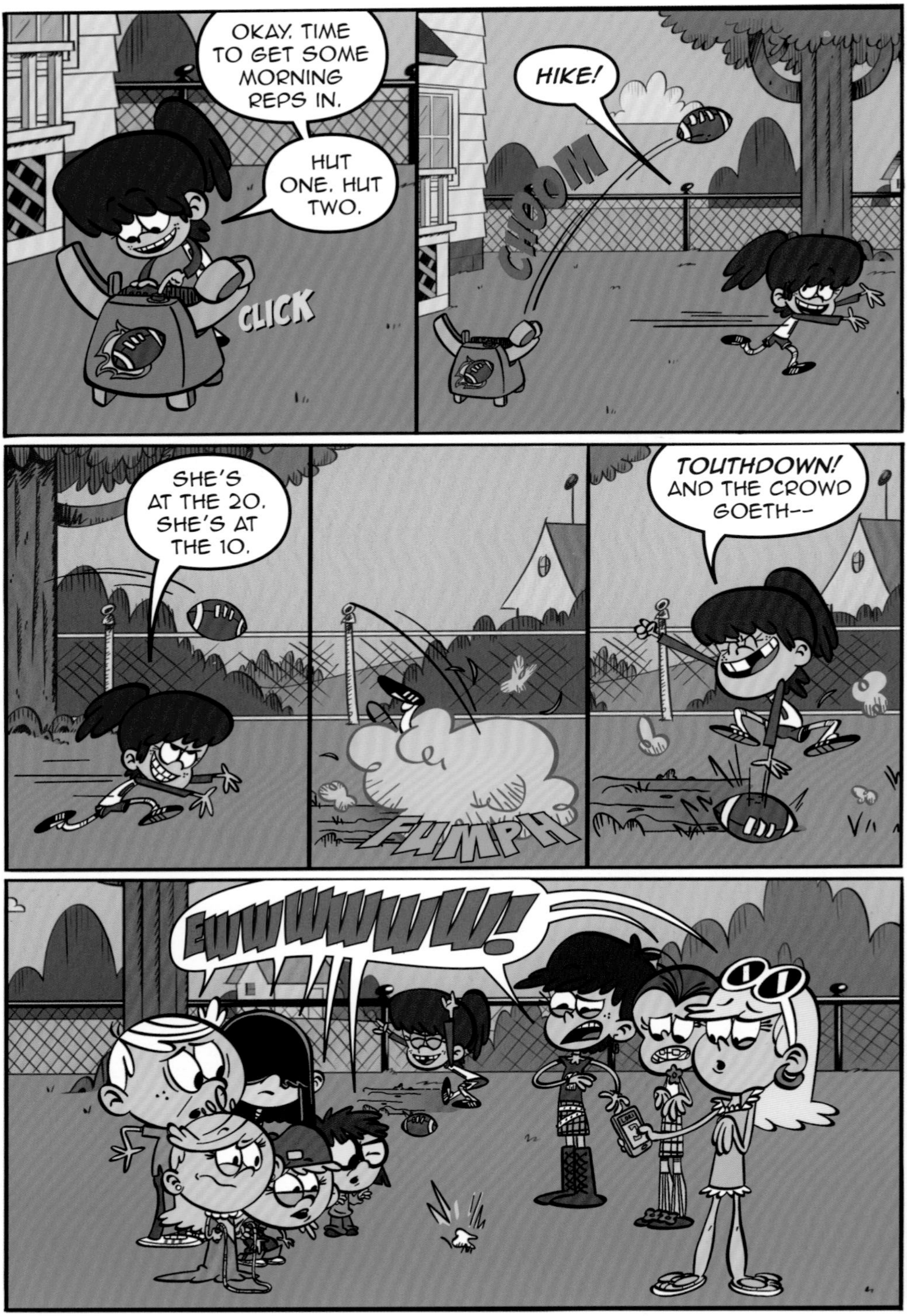
OKAY. TIME TO GET SOME MORNING REPS IN.
HUT ONE. HUT TWO.
CLICK
HIKE!
CHOOOM
SHE'S AT THE 20. SHE'S AT THE 10.
FUMPH
TOUTHDOWN! AND THE CROWD GOETH--
EWWWWWW!

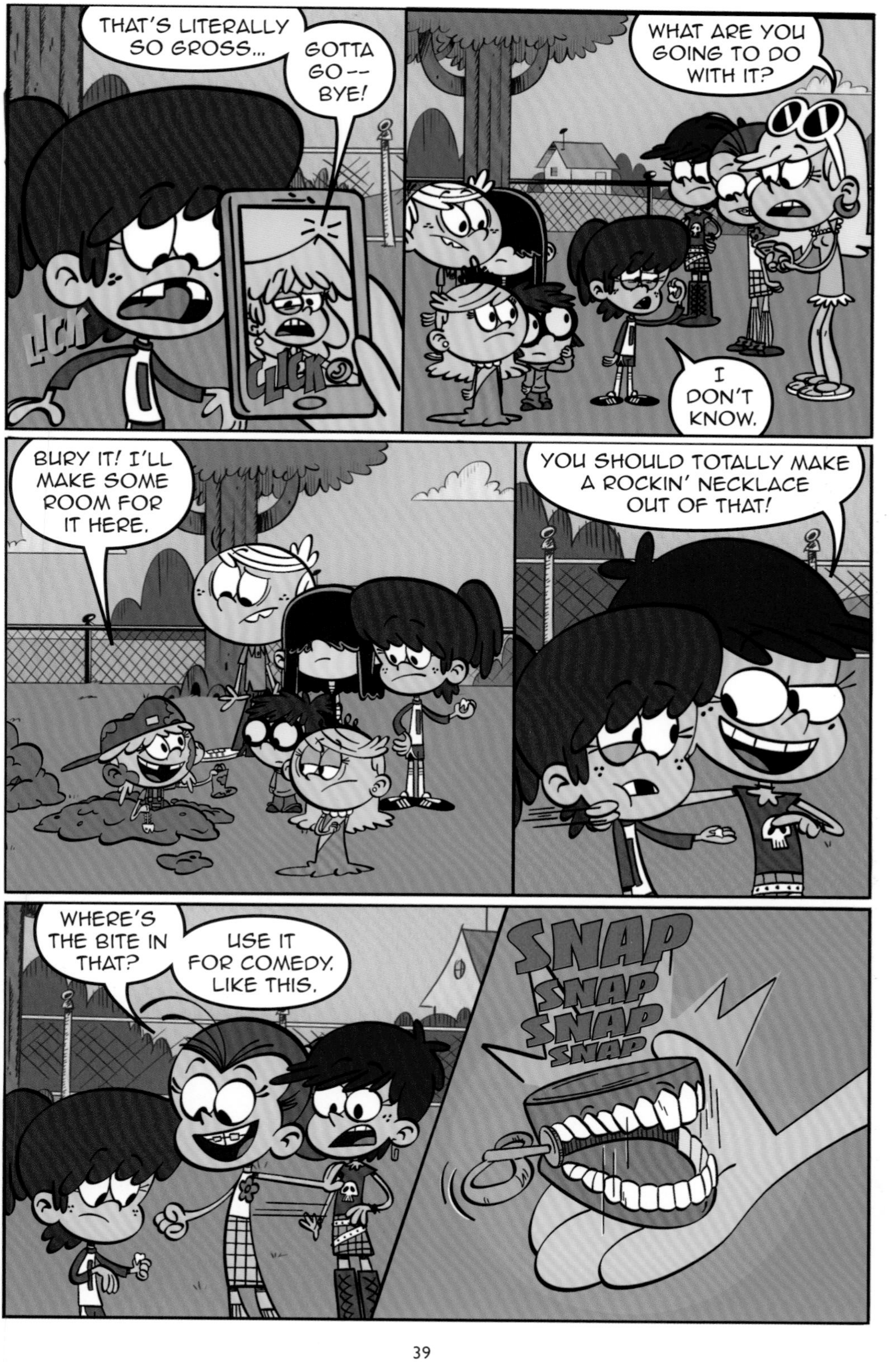
THAT'S LITERALLY SO GROSS...
GOTTA GO-- BYE!
CLICK
CLICK
WHAT ARE YOU GOING TO DO WITH IT?
I DON'T KNOW.
BURY IT! I'LL MAKE SOME ROOM FOR IT HERE.
YOU SHOULD TOTALLY MAKE A ROCKIN' NECKLACE OUT OF THAT!
WHERE'S THE BITE IN THAT?
USE IT FOR COMEDY. LIKE THIS.
SNAP
SNAP
SNAP
SNAP

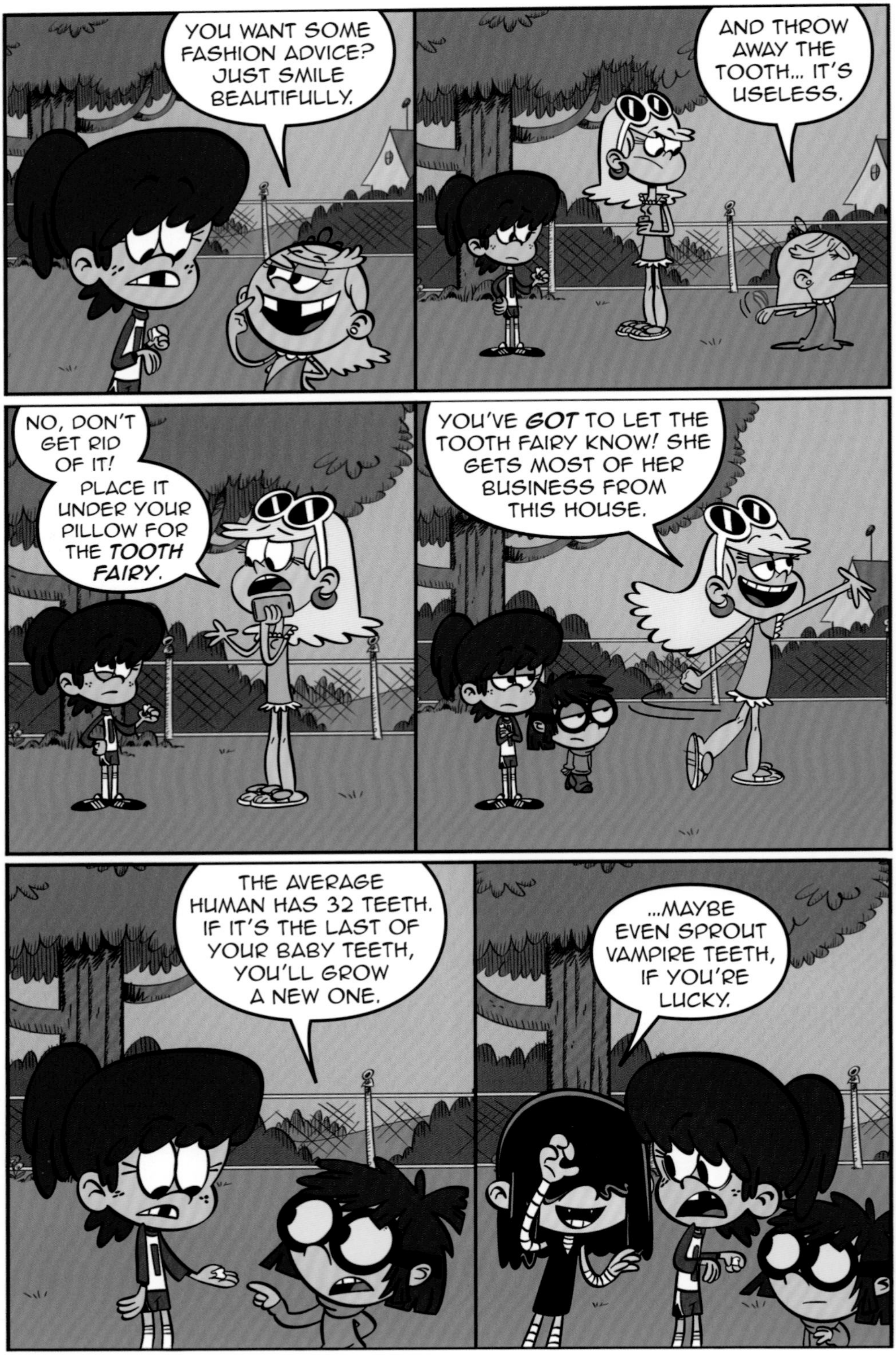
YOU WANT SOME FASHION ADVICE? JUST SMILE BEAUTIFULLY.
AND THROW AWAY THE TOOTH... IT'S USELESS.
NO, DON'T GET RID OF IT!
PLACE IT UNDER YOUR PILLOW FOR THE TOOTH FAIRY.
YOU'VE GOT TO LET THE TOOTH FAIRY KNOW! SHE GETS MOST OF HER BUSINESS FROM THIS HOUSE.
THE AVERAGE HUMAN HAS 32 TEETH. IF IT'S THE LAST OF YOUR BABY TEETH, YOU'LL GROW A NEW ONE.
...MAYBE EVEN SPROUT VAMPIRE TEETH, IF YOU'RE LUCKY.

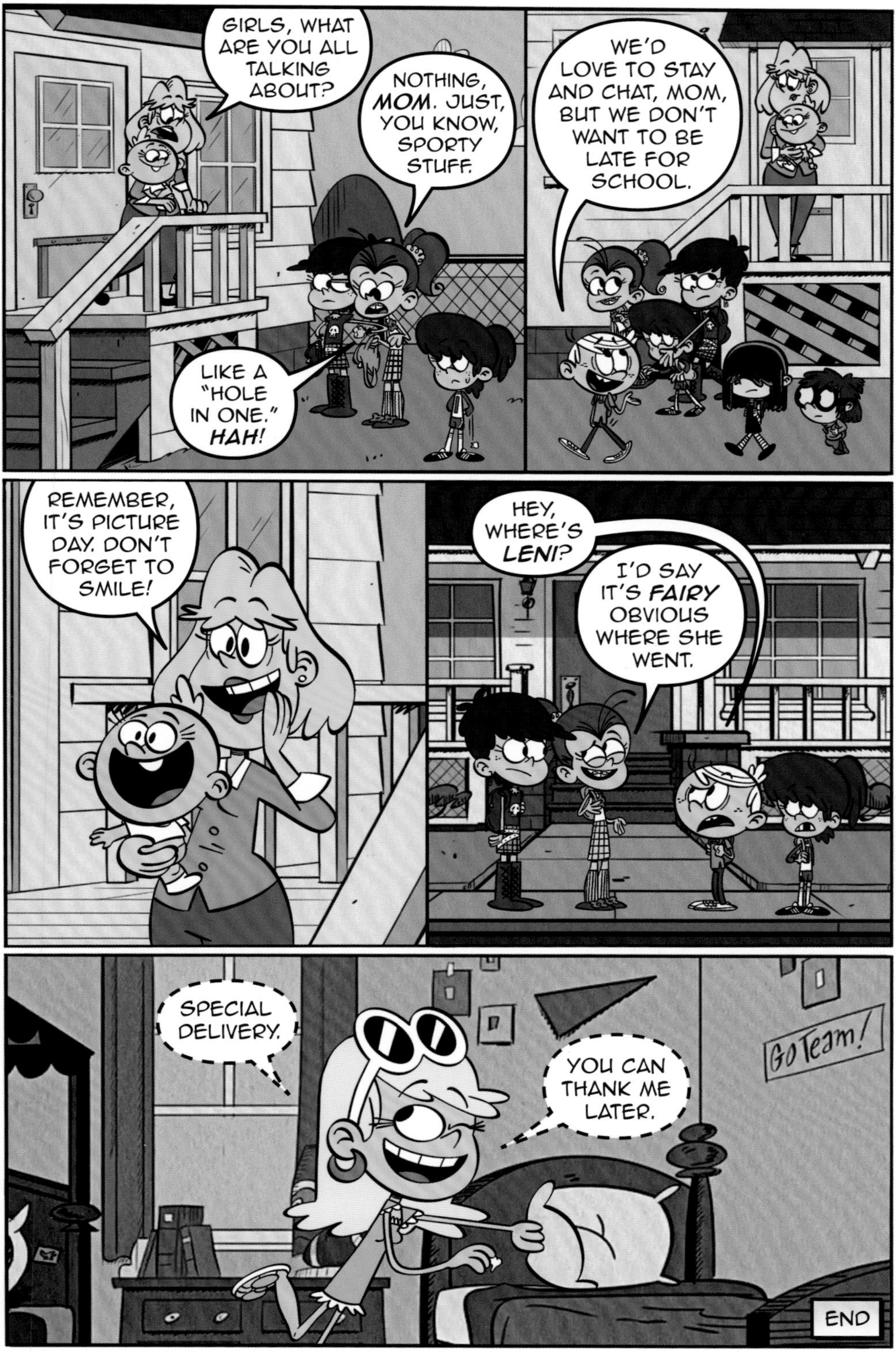

GIRLS, WHAT ARE YOU ALL TALKING ABOUT?
NOTHING, **MOM**. JUST, YOU KNOW, SPORTY STUFF.
LIKE A "HOLE IN ONE." **HAH**!
WE'D LOVE TO STAY AND CHAT, MOM, BUT WE DON'T WANT TO BE LATE FOR SCHOOL.
REMEMBER, IT'S PICTURE DAY. DON'T FORGET TO SMILE!
HEY, WHERE'S **LENI**?
I'D SAY IT'S **FAIRY** OBVIOUS WHERE SHE WENT.
SPECIAL DELIVERY.
YOU CAN THANK ME LATER.
Go Team!
END

"ONE MAN CROW"

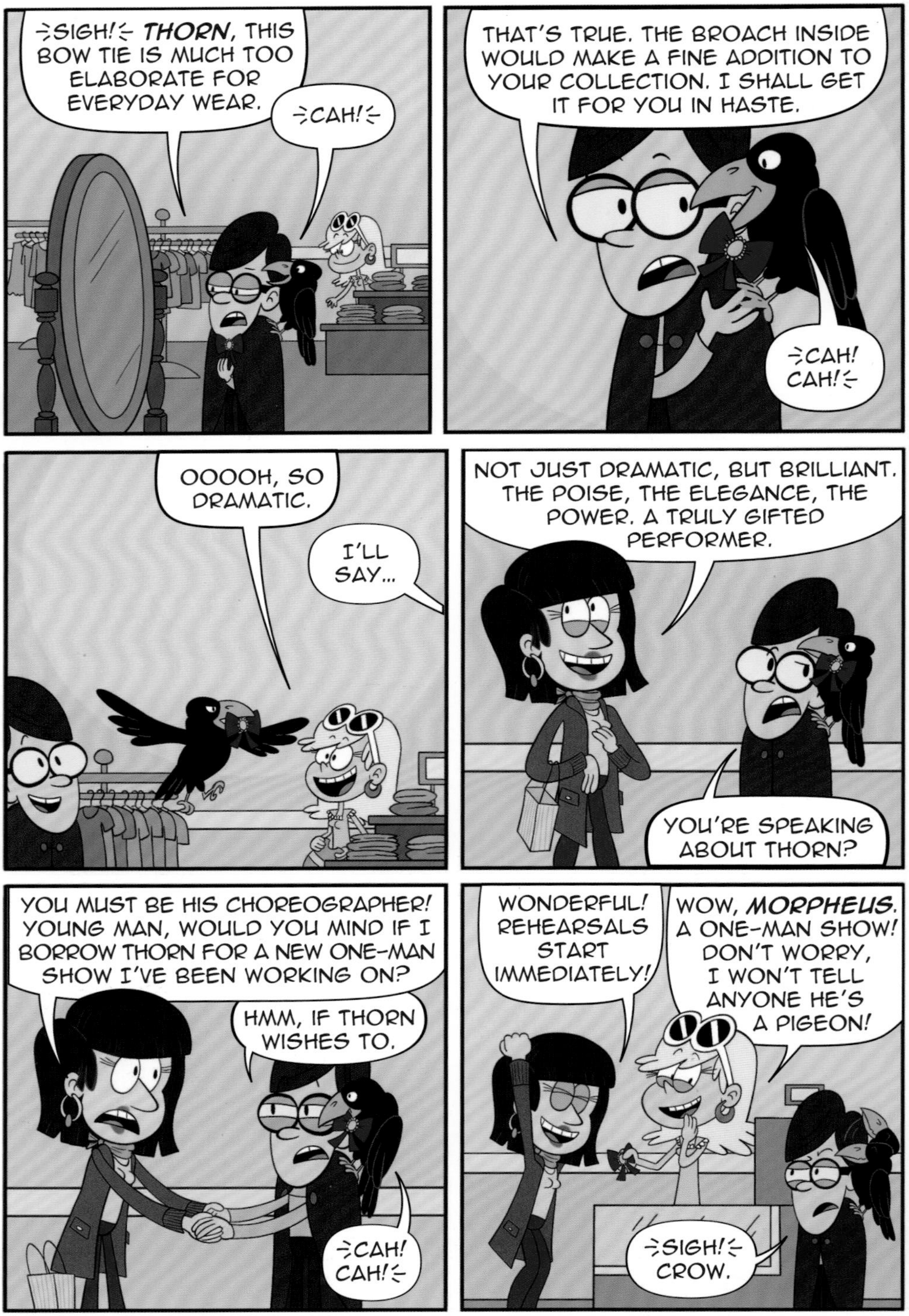

~SIGH!~ THORN, THIS BOW TIE IS MUCH TOO ELABORATE FOR EVERYDAY WEAR.
~CAH!~
THAT'S TRUE. THE BROACH INSIDE WOULD MAKE A FINE ADDITION TO YOUR COLLECTION. I SHALL GET IT FOR YOU IN HASTE.
~CAH! CAH!~
OOOOH, SO DRAMATIC.
I'LL SAY...
NOT JUST DRAMATIC, BUT BRILLIANT. THE POISE, THE ELEGANCE, THE POWER. A TRULY GIFTED PERFORMER.
YOU'RE SPEAKING ABOUT THORN?
YOU MUST BE HIS CHOREOGRAPHER! YOUNG MAN, WOULD YOU MIND IF I BORROW THORN FOR A NEW ONE-MAN SHOW I'VE BEEN WORKING ON?
HMM, IF THORN WISHES TO.
~CAH! CAH!~
WONDERFUL! REHEARSALS START IMMEDIATELY!
WOW, MORPHEUS. A ONE-MAN SHOW! DON'T WORRY, I WON'T TELL ANYONE HE'S A PIGEON!
~SIGH!~ CROW.

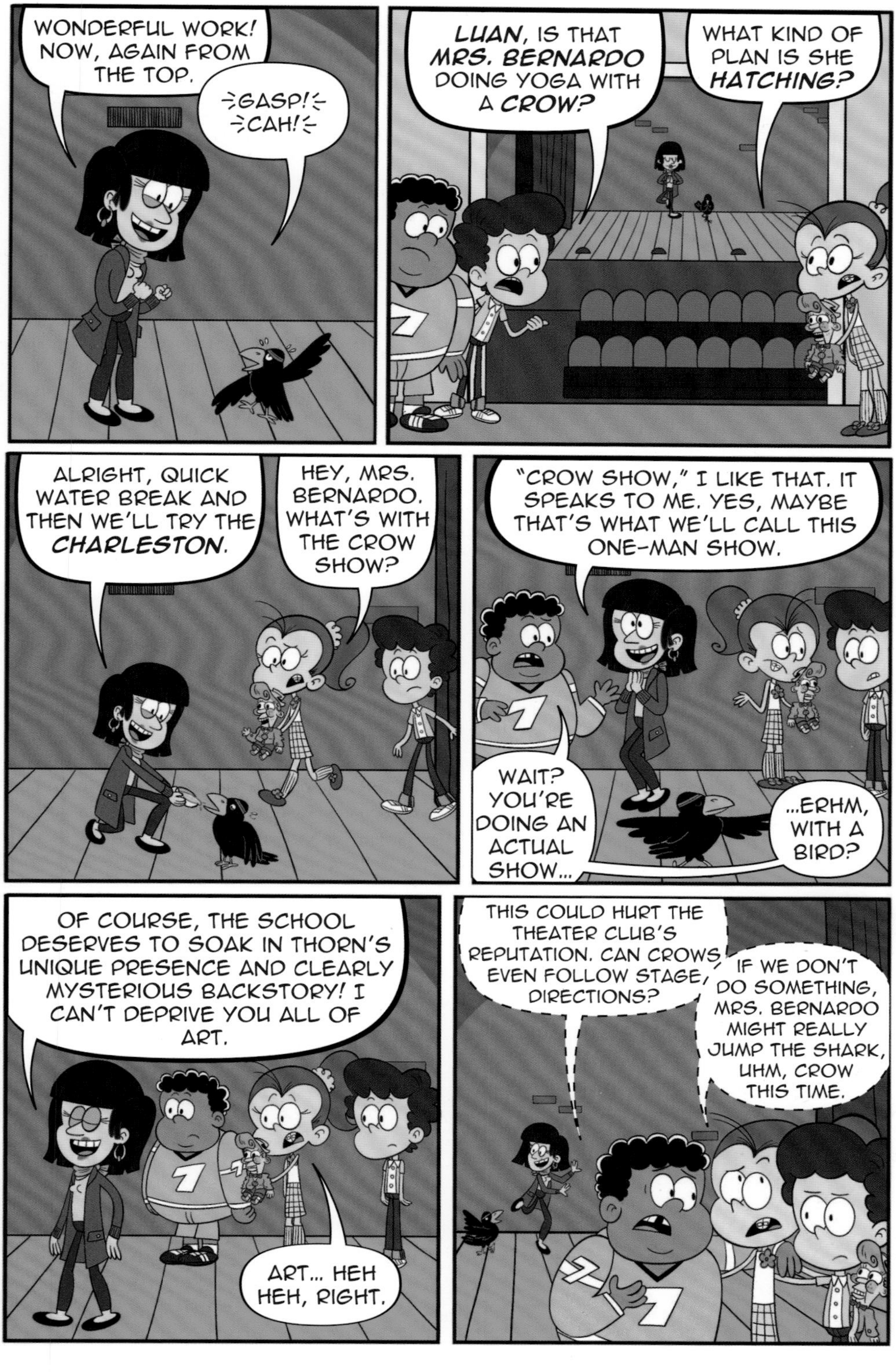
WONDERFUL WORK! NOW, AGAIN FROM THE TOP.
GASP! CAH!
LUAN, IS THAT MRS. BERNARDO DOING YOGA WITH A CROW?
WHAT KIND OF PLAN IS SHE HATCHING?
ALRIGHT, QUICK WATER BREAK AND THEN WE'LL TRY THE CHARLESTON.
HEY, MRS. BERNARDO. WHAT'S WITH THE CROW SHOW?
"CROW SHOW," I LIKE THAT. IT SPEAKS TO ME. YES, MAYBE THAT'S WHAT WE'LL CALL THIS ONE-MAN SHOW.
WAIT? YOU'RE DOING AN ACTUAL SHOW...
...ERHM, WITH A BIRD?
OF COURSE, THE SCHOOL DESERVES TO SOAK IN THORN'S UNIQUE PRESENCE AND CLEARLY MYSTERIOUS BACKSTORY! I CAN'T DEPRIVE YOU ALL OF ART.
ART... HEH HEH, RIGHT.
THIS COULD HURT THE THEATER CLUB'S REPUTATION. CAN CROWS EVEN FOLLOW STAGE DIRECTIONS?
IF WE DON'T DO SOMETHING, MRS. BERNARDO MIGHT REALLY JUMP THE SHARK, UHM, CROW THIS TIME.

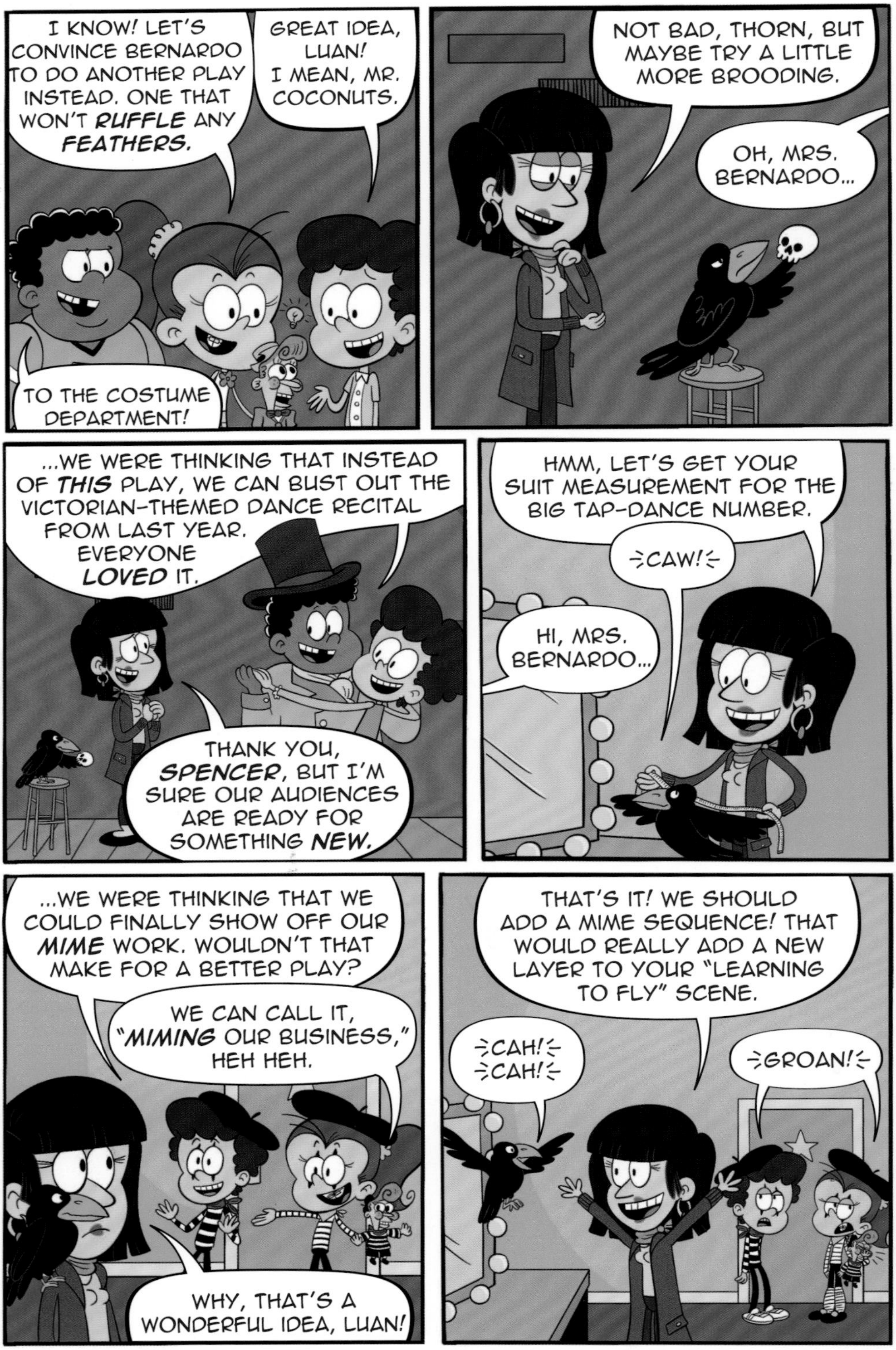
I KNOW! LET'S CONVINCE BERNARDO TO DO ANOTHER PLAY INSTEAD. ONE THAT WON'T RUFFLE ANY FEATHERS.
GREAT IDEA, LUAN! I MEAN, MR. COCONUTS.
TO THE COSTUME DEPARTMENT!
NOT BAD, THORN, BUT MAYBE TRY A LITTLE MORE BROODING.
OH, MRS. BERNARDO...
...WE WERE THINKING THAT INSTEAD OF THIS PLAY, WE CAN BUST OUT THE VICTORIAN-THEMED DANCE RECITAL FROM LAST YEAR. EVERYONE LOVED IT.
THANK YOU, SPENCER, BUT I'M SURE OUR AUDIENCES ARE READY FOR SOMETHING NEW.
HMM, LET'S GET YOUR SUIT MEASUREMENT FOR THE BIG TAP-DANCE NUMBER.
CAW!
HI, MRS. BERNARDO...
...WE WERE THINKING THAT WE COULD FINALLY SHOW OFF OUR MIME WORK. WOULDN'T THAT MAKE FOR A BETTER PLAY?
WE CAN CALL IT, "MIMING OUR BUSINESS," HEH HEH.
WHY, THAT'S A WONDERFUL IDEA, LUAN!
THAT'S IT! WE SHOULD ADD A MIME SEQUENCE! THAT WOULD REALLY ADD A NEW LAYER TO YOUR "LEARNING TO FLY" SCENE.
CAH! CAH!
GROAN!

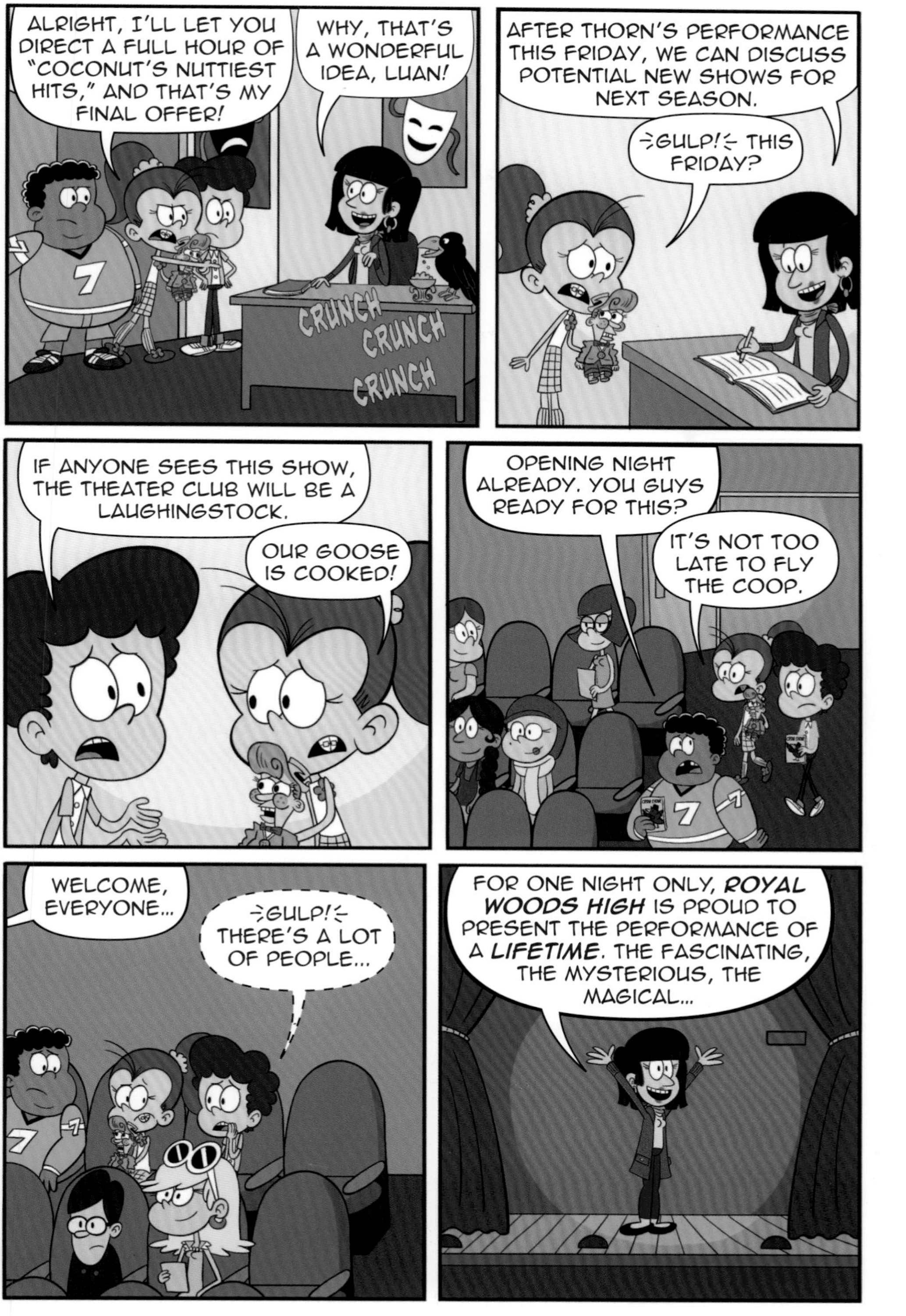
ALRIGHT, I'LL LET YOU DIRECT A FULL HOUR OF "COCONUT'S NUTTIEST HITS," AND THAT'S MY FINAL OFFER!
WHY, THAT'S A WONDERFUL IDEA, LUAN!
CRUNCH CRUNCH CRUNCH
AFTER THORN'S PERFORMANCE THIS FRIDAY, WE CAN DISCUSS POTENTIAL NEW SHOWS FOR NEXT SEASON.
GULP! THIS FRIDAY?
IF ANYONE SEES THIS SHOW, THE THEATER CLUB WILL BE A LAUGHINGSTOCK.
OUR GOOSE IS COOKED!
OPENING NIGHT ALREADY. YOU GUYS READY FOR THIS?
IT'S NOT TOO LATE TO FLY THE COOP.
WELCOME, EVERYONE...
GULP! THERE'S A LOT OF PEOPLE...
FOR ONE NIGHT ONLY, *ROYAL WOODS HIGH* IS PROUD TO PRESENT THE PERFORMANCE OF A *LIFETIME*. THE FASCINATING, THE MYSTERIOUS, THE MAGICAL...

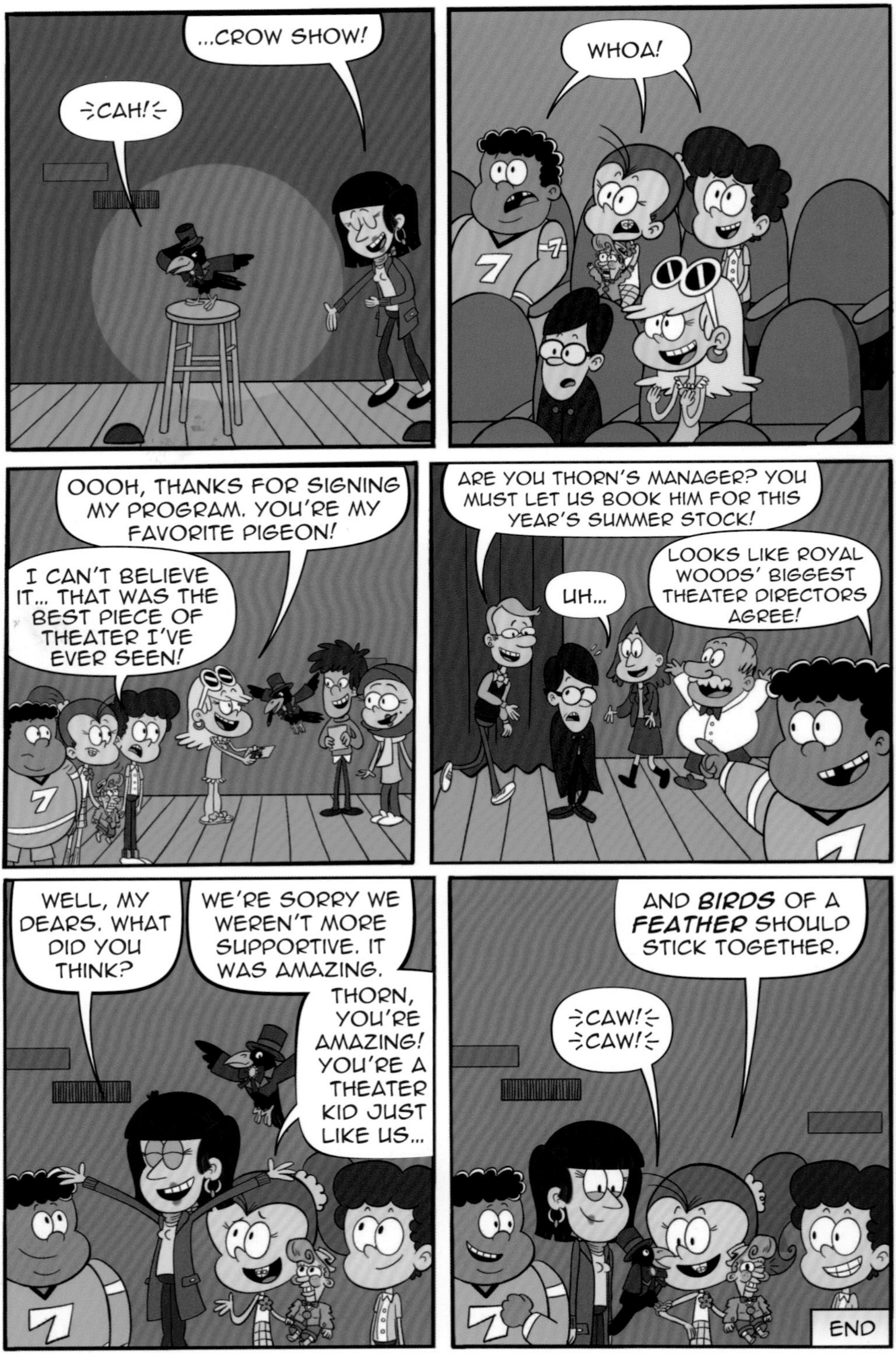

...CROW SHOW!
CAH!
WHOA!
OOOH, THANKS FOR SIGNING MY PROGRAM. YOU'RE MY FAVORITE PIGEON!
I CAN'T BELIEVE IT... THAT WAS THE BEST PIECE OF THEATER I'VE EVER SEEN!
ARE YOU THORN'S MANAGER? YOU MUST LET US BOOK HIM FOR THIS YEAR'S SUMMER STOCK!
UH...
LOOKS LIKE ROYAL WOODS' BIGGEST THEATER DIRECTORS AGREE!
WELL, MY DEARS. WHAT DID YOU THINK?
WE'RE SORRY WE WEREN'T MORE SUPPORTIVE. IT WAS AMAZING.
THORN, YOU'RE AMAZING! YOU'RE A THEATER KID JUST LIKE US...
AND BIRDS OF A FEATHER SHOULD STICK TOGETHER.
CAW! CAW!
END

"MOO-MENTO"

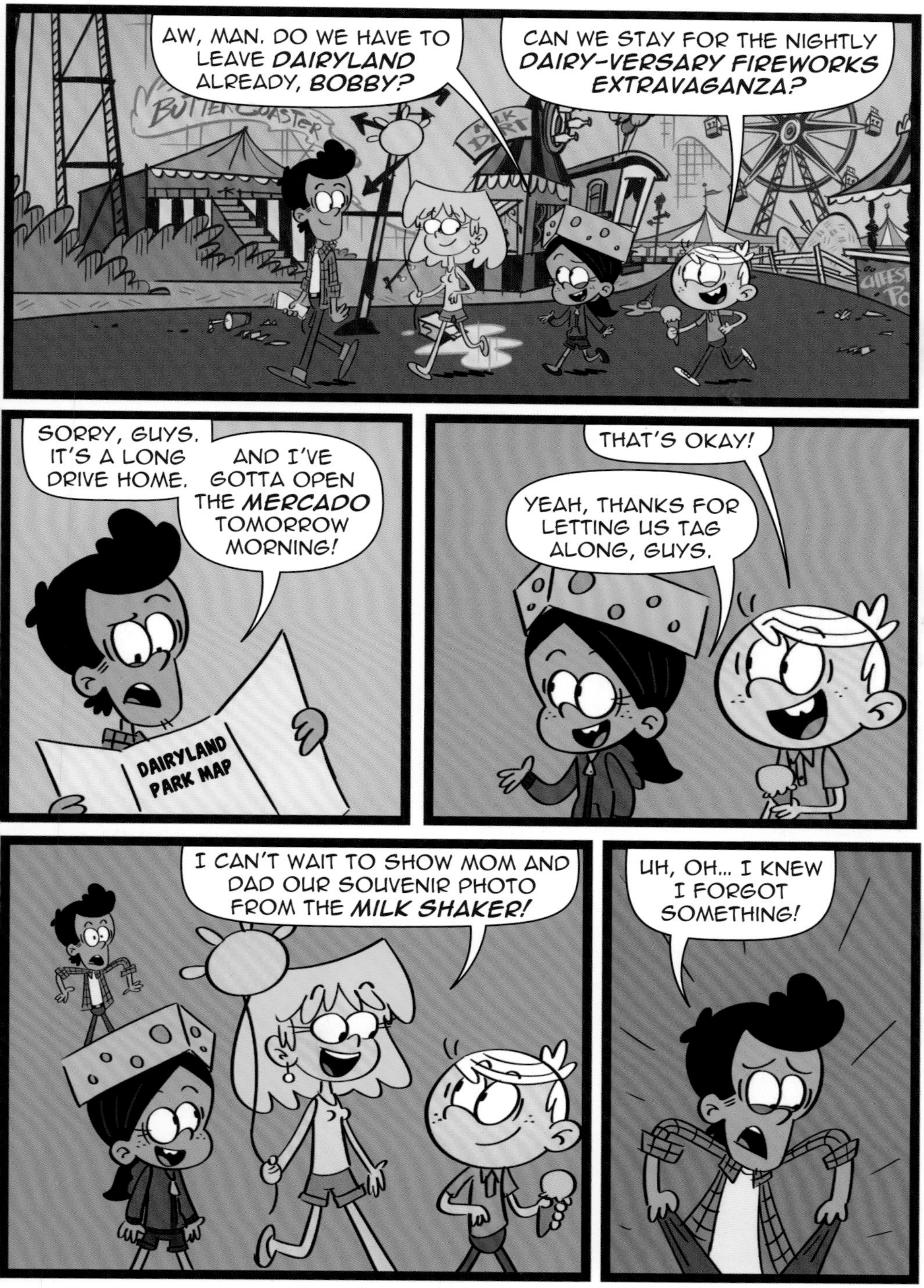
AW, MAN. DO WE HAVE TO LEAVE DAIRYLAND ALREADY, BOBBY?
CAN WE STAY FOR THE NIGHTLY DAIRY-VERSARY FIREWORKS EXTRAVAGANZA?
SORRY, GUYS. IT'S A LONG DRIVE HOME.
AND I'VE GOTTA OPEN THE MERCADO TOMORROW MORNING!
DAIRYLAND PARK MAP
THAT'S OKAY!
YEAH, THANKS FOR LETTING US TAG ALONG, GUYS.
I CAN'T WAIT TO SHOW MOM AND DAD OUR SOUVENIR PHOTO FROM THE MILK SHAKER!
UH, OH... I KNEW I FORGOT SOMETHING!

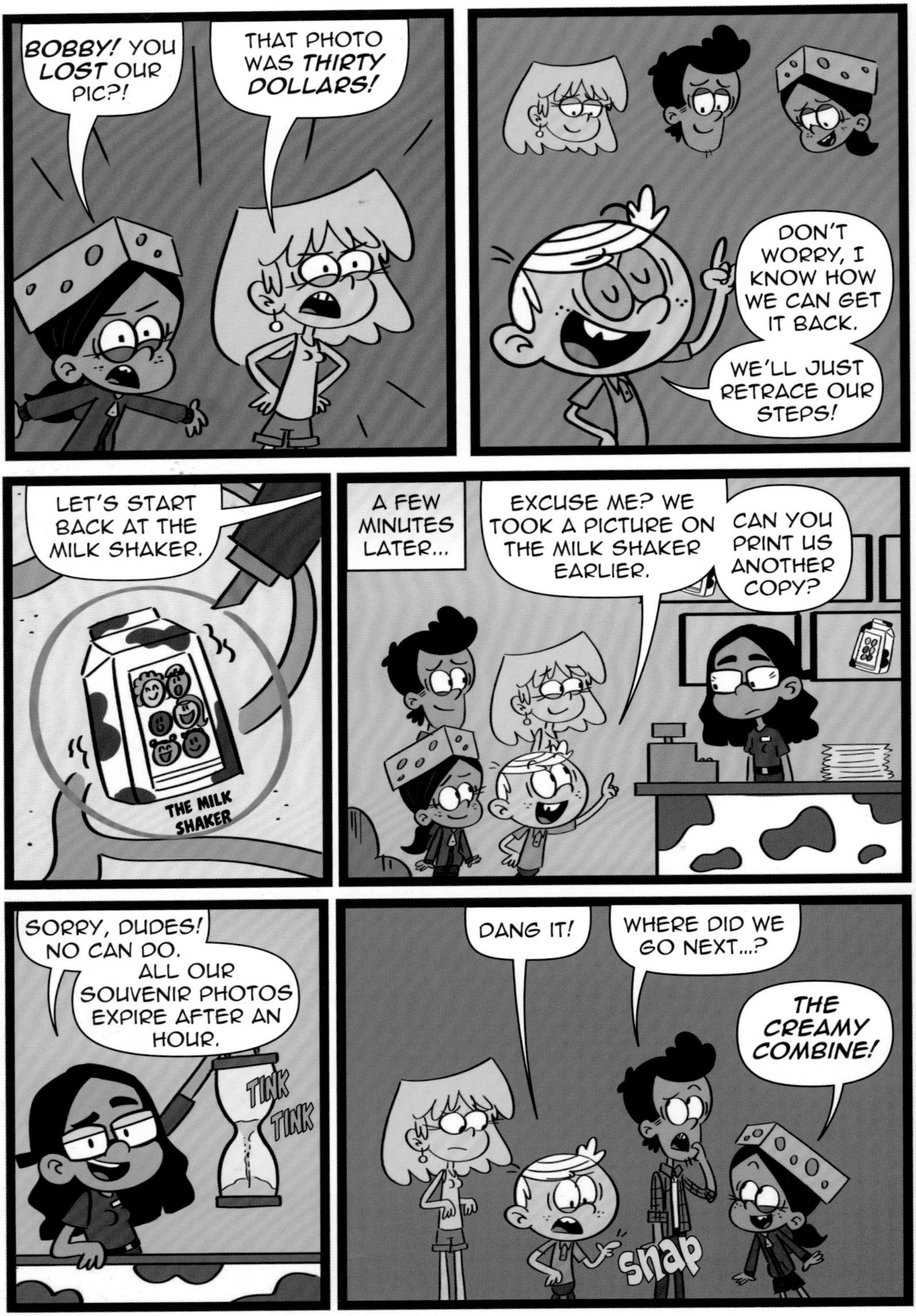

BOBBY! YOU ***LOST*** OUR PIC?!
THAT PHOTO WAS ***THIRTY DOLLARS!***
DON'T WORRY, I KNOW HOW WE CAN GET IT BACK.
WE'LL JUST RETRACE OUR STEPS!
LET'S START BACK AT THE MILK SHAKER.
THE MILK SHAKER
A FEW MINUTES LATER...
EXCUSE ME? WE TOOK A PICTURE ON THE MILK SHAKER EARLIER.
CAN YOU PRINT US ANOTHER COPY?
SORRY, DUDES! NO CAN DO.
ALL OUR SOUVENIR PHOTOS EXPIRE AFTER AN HOUR.
TINK
TINK
DANG IT!
WHERE DID WE GO NEXT...?
THE CREAMY COMBINE!
SNAP

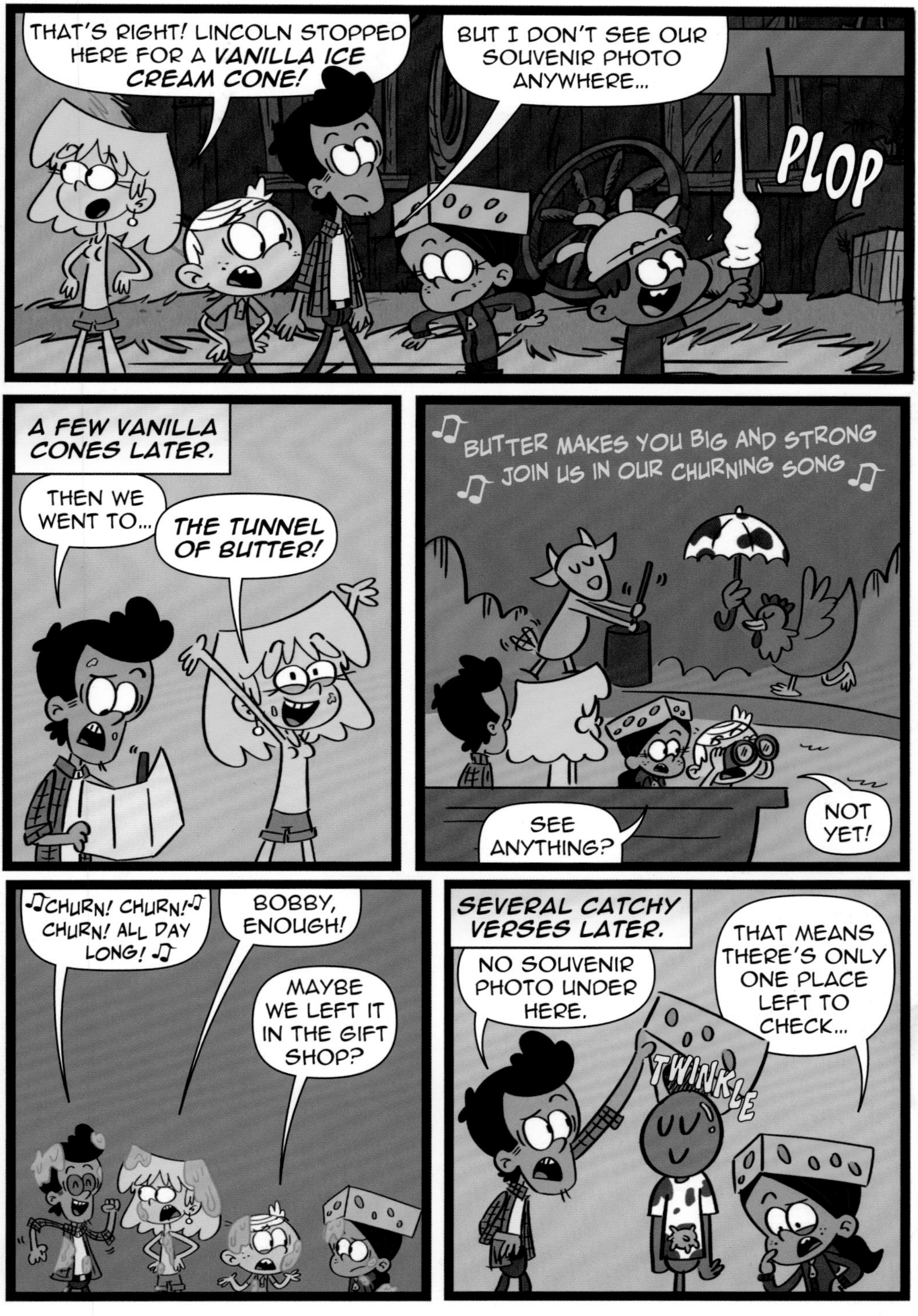
THAT'S RIGHT! LINCOLN STOPPED HERE FOR A VANILLA ICE CREAM CONE!
BUT I DON'T SEE OUR SOUVENIR PHOTO ANYWHERE...
PLOP
A FEW VANILLA CONES LATER.
THEN WE WENT TO...
THE TUNNEL OF BUTTER!
♫ BUTTER MAKES YOU BIG AND STRONG
♫ JOIN US IN OUR CHURNING SONG ♫
SEE ANYTHING?
NOT YET!
♫CHURN! CHURN!♫ CHURN! ALL DAY LONG! ♫
BOBBY, ENOUGH!
MAYBE WE LEFT IT IN THE GIFT SHOP?
SEVERAL CATCHY VERSES LATER.
NO SOUVENIR PHOTO UNDER HERE.
TWINKLE
THAT MEANS THERE'S ONLY ONE PLACE LEFT TO CHECK...

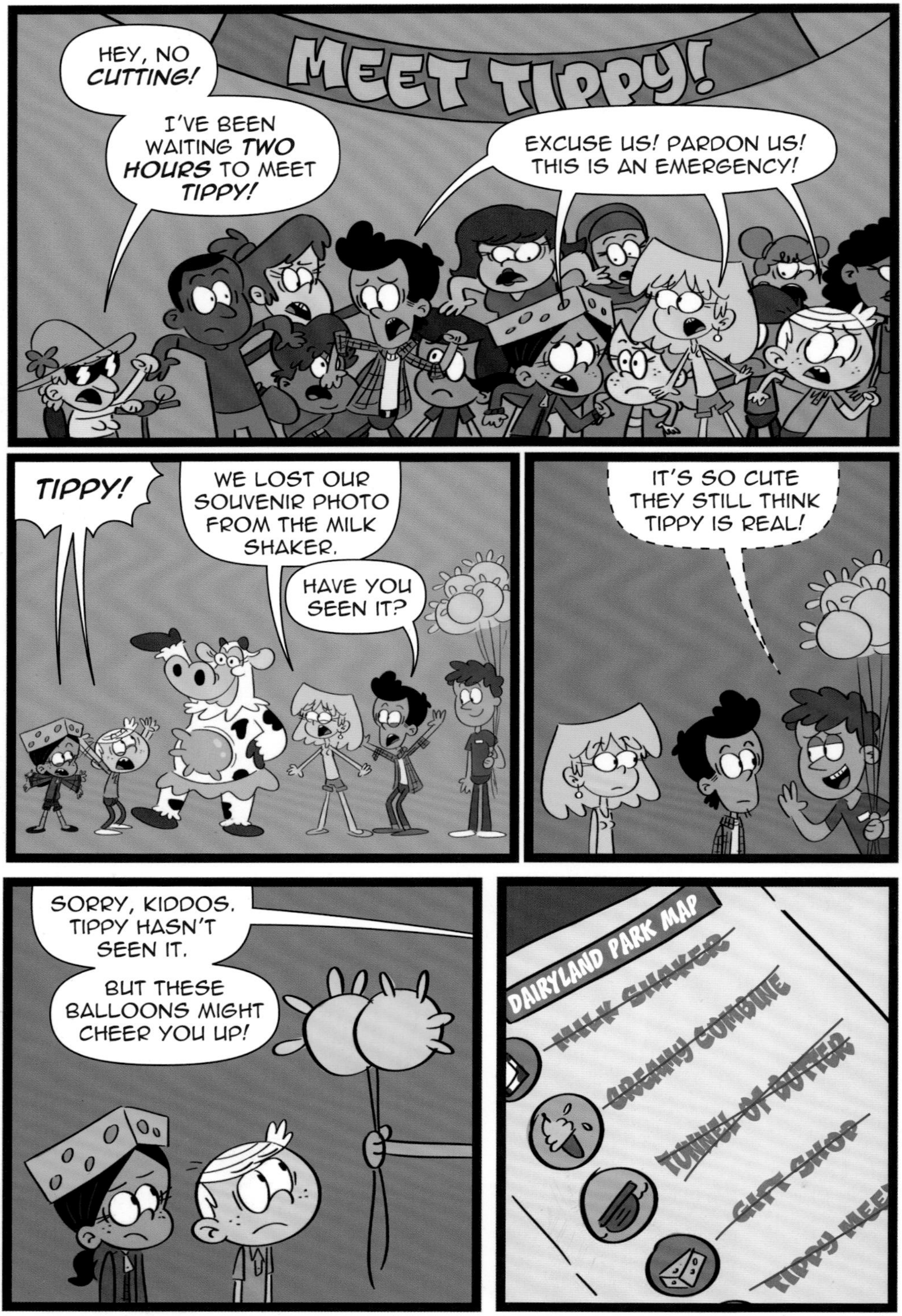
MEET TIPPY!
HEY, NO CUTTING!
I'VE BEEN WAITING TWO HOURS TO MEET TIPPY!
EXCUSE US! PARDON US! THIS IS AN EMERGENCY!
TIPPY!
WE LOST OUR SOUVENIR PHOTO FROM THE MILK SHAKER.
HAVE YOU SEEN IT?
IT'S SO CUTE THEY STILL THINK TIPPY IS REAL!
SORRY, KIDDOS. TIPPY HASN'T SEEN IT.
BUT THESE BALLOONS MIGHT CHEER YOU UP!
DAIRYLAND PARK MAP
MILK SHAKER
CREAMY COMBINE
TUNNEL OF BUTTER
GIFT SHOP
TIPPY MEE

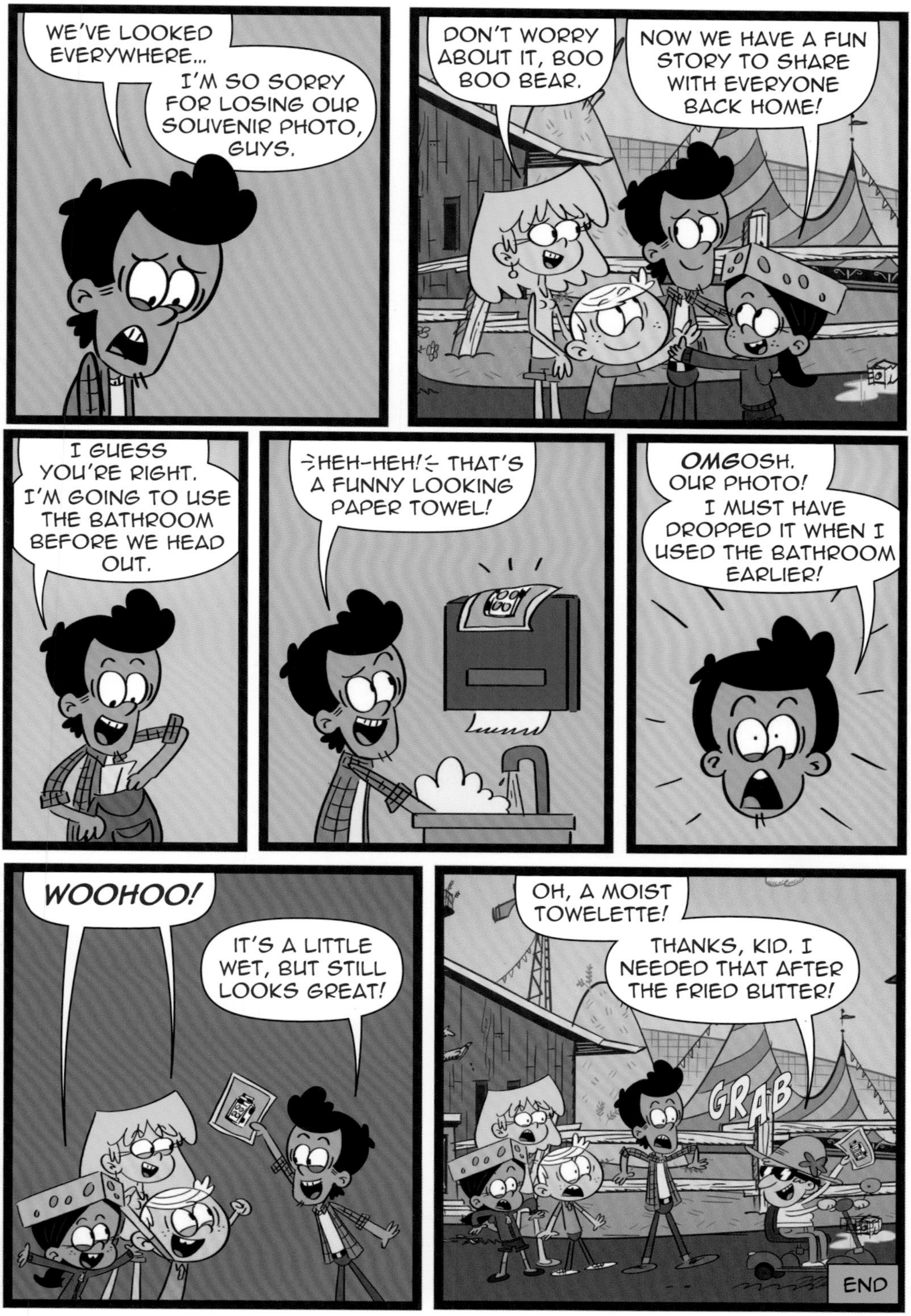
WE'VE LOOKED EVERYWHERE...
I'M SO SORRY FOR LOSING OUR SOUVENIR PHOTO, GUYS.
DON'T WORRY ABOUT IT, BOO BOO BEAR.
NOW WE HAVE A FUN STORY TO SHARE WITH EVERYONE BACK HOME!
I GUESS YOU'RE RIGHT. I'M GOING TO USE THE BATHROOM BEFORE WE HEAD OUT.
HEH-HEH! THAT'S A FUNNY LOOKING PAPER TOWEL!
OMGOSH. OUR PHOTO!
I MUST HAVE DROPPED IT WHEN I USED THE BATHROOM EARLIER!
WOOHOO!
IT'S A LITTLE WET, BUT STILL LOOKS GREAT!
OH, A MOIST TOWELETTE!
THANKS, KID. I NEEDED THAT AFTER THE FRIED BUTTER!
GRAB
END

“BARN OF HORRORS”

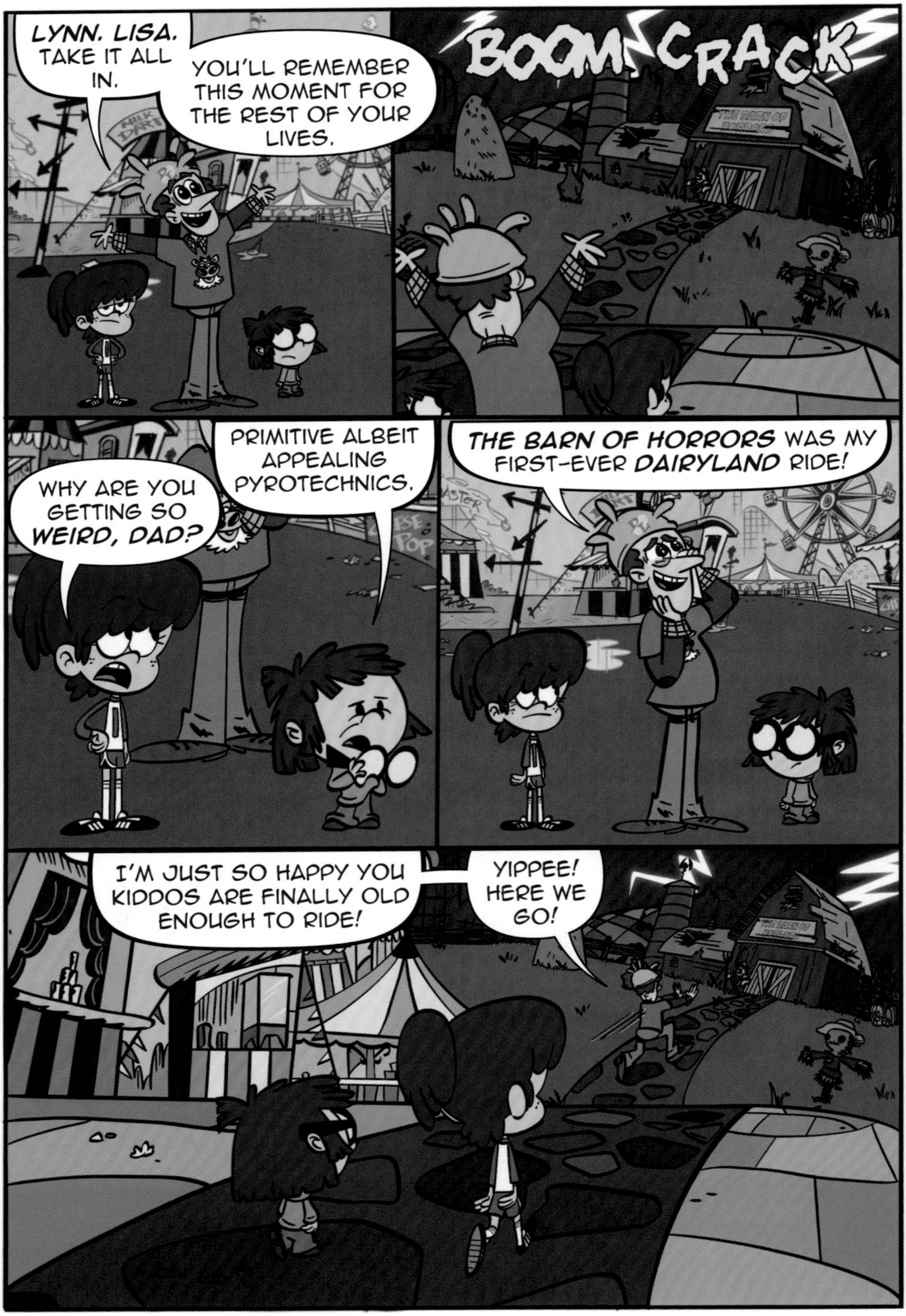

LYNN. LISA. TAKE IT ALL IN.
YOU'LL REMEMBER THIS MOMENT FOR THE REST OF YOUR LIVES.
BOOM
CRACK
THE BARN OF HORRORS
WHY ARE YOU GETTING SO WEIRD, DAD?
PRIMITIVE ALBEIT APPEALING PYROTECHNICS.
THE BARN OF HORRORS WAS MY FIRST-EVER DAIRYLAND RIDE!
I'M JUST SO HAPPY YOU KIDDOS ARE FINALLY OLD ENOUGH TO RIDE!
YIPPEE! HERE WE GO!

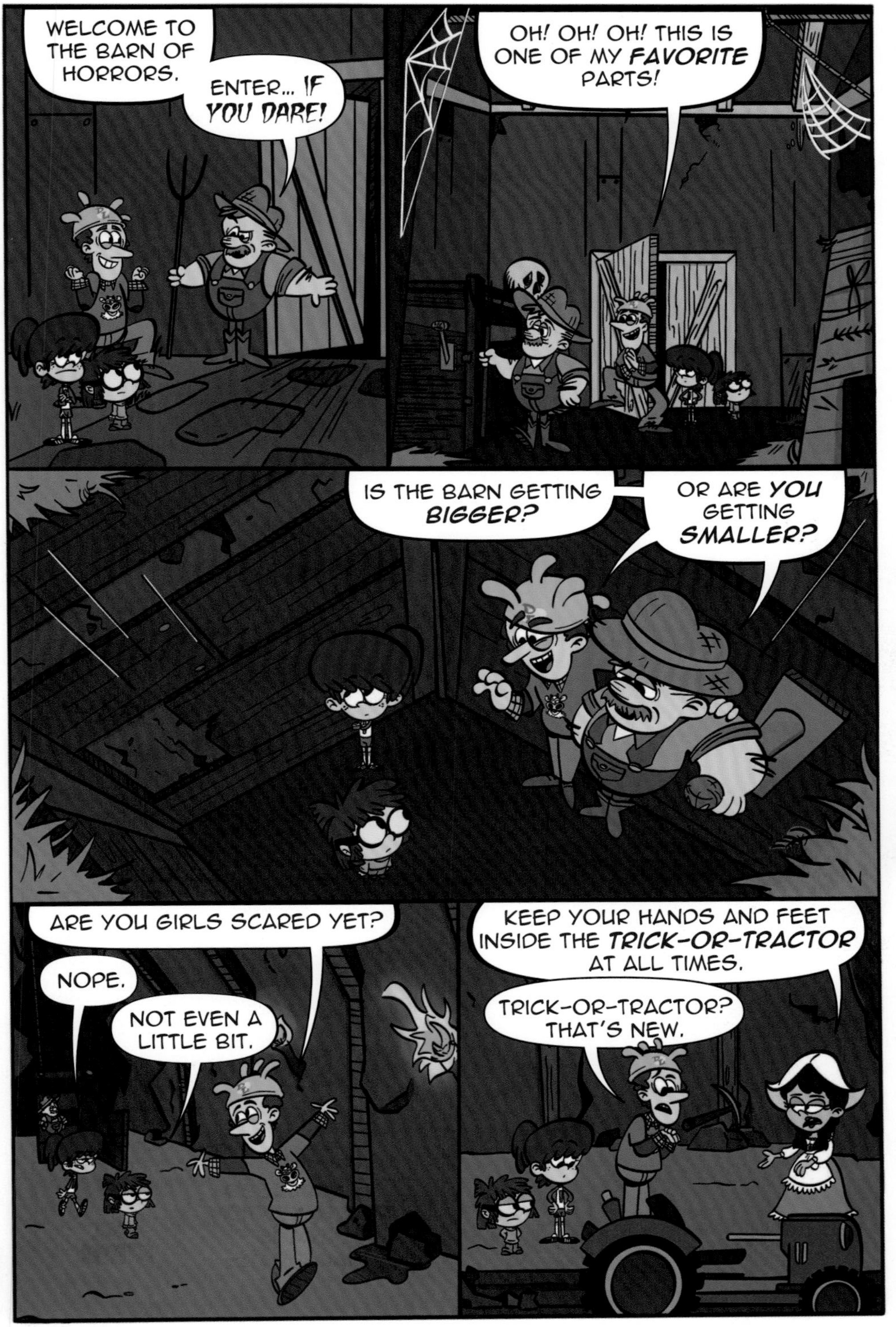

WELCOME TO THE BARN OF HORRORS.
ENTER... IF *YOU DARE!*
OH! OH! OH! THIS IS ONE OF MY ***FAVORITE*** PARTS!
IS THE BARN GETTING ***BIGGER?***
OR ARE ***YOU*** GETTING ***SMALLER?***
ARE YOU GIRLS SCARED YET?
NOPE.
NOT EVEN A LITTLE BIT.
KEEP YOUR HANDS AND FEET INSIDE THE ***TRICK-OR-TRACTOR*** AT ALL TIMES.
TRICK-OR-TRACTOR? THAT'S NEW.

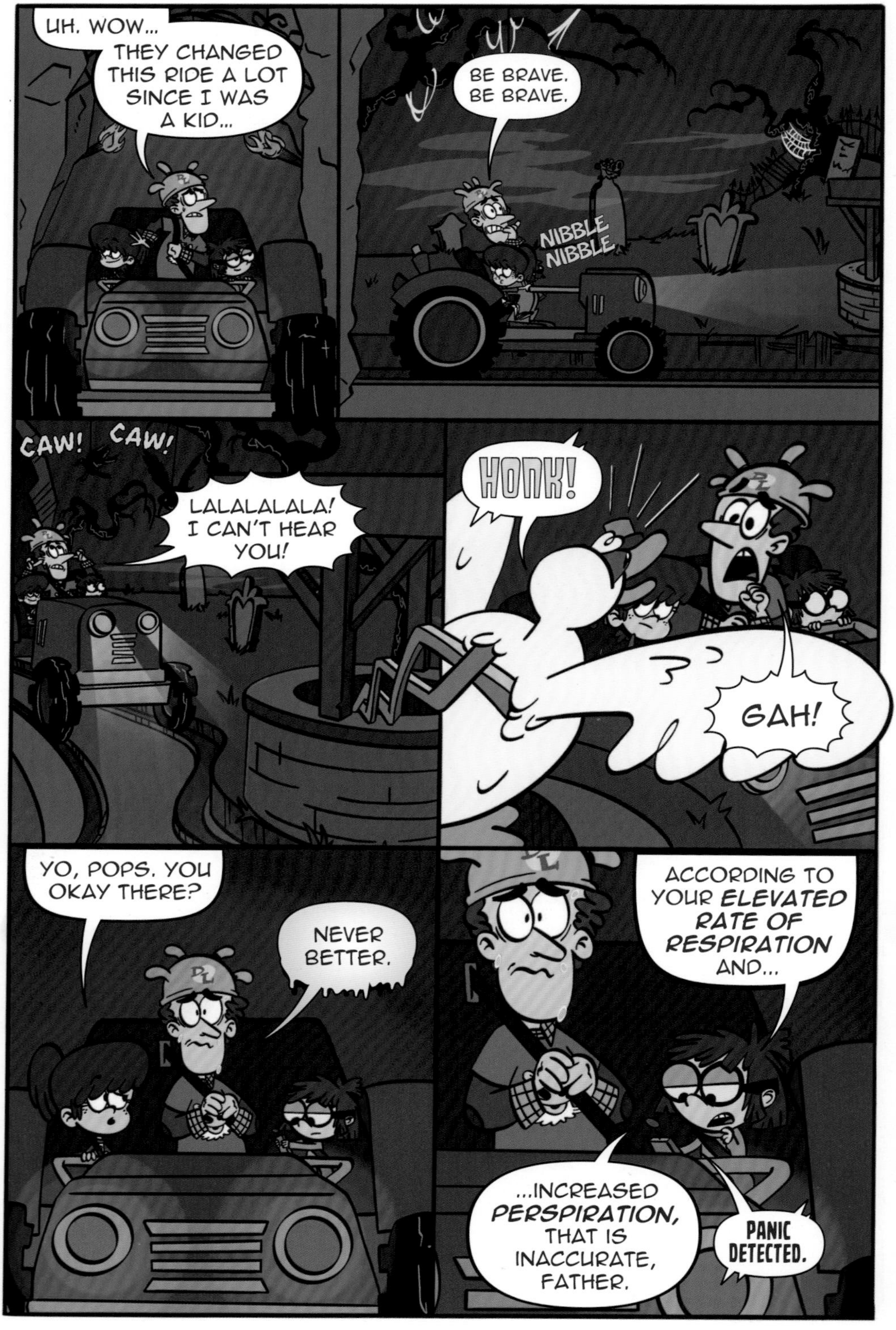
UH. WOW...
THEY CHANGED THIS RIDE A LOT SINCE I WAS A KID...
BE BRAVE. BE BRAVE.
NIBBLE NIBBLE
CAW! CAW!
LALALALALA! I CAN'T HEAR YOU!
HONK!
GAH!
YO, POPS. YOU OKAY THERE?
NEVER BETTER.
ACCORDING TO YOUR *ELEVATED RATE OF RESPIRATION* AND...
...INCREASED *PERSPIRATION*, THAT IS INACCURATE, FATHER.
PANIC DETECTED.

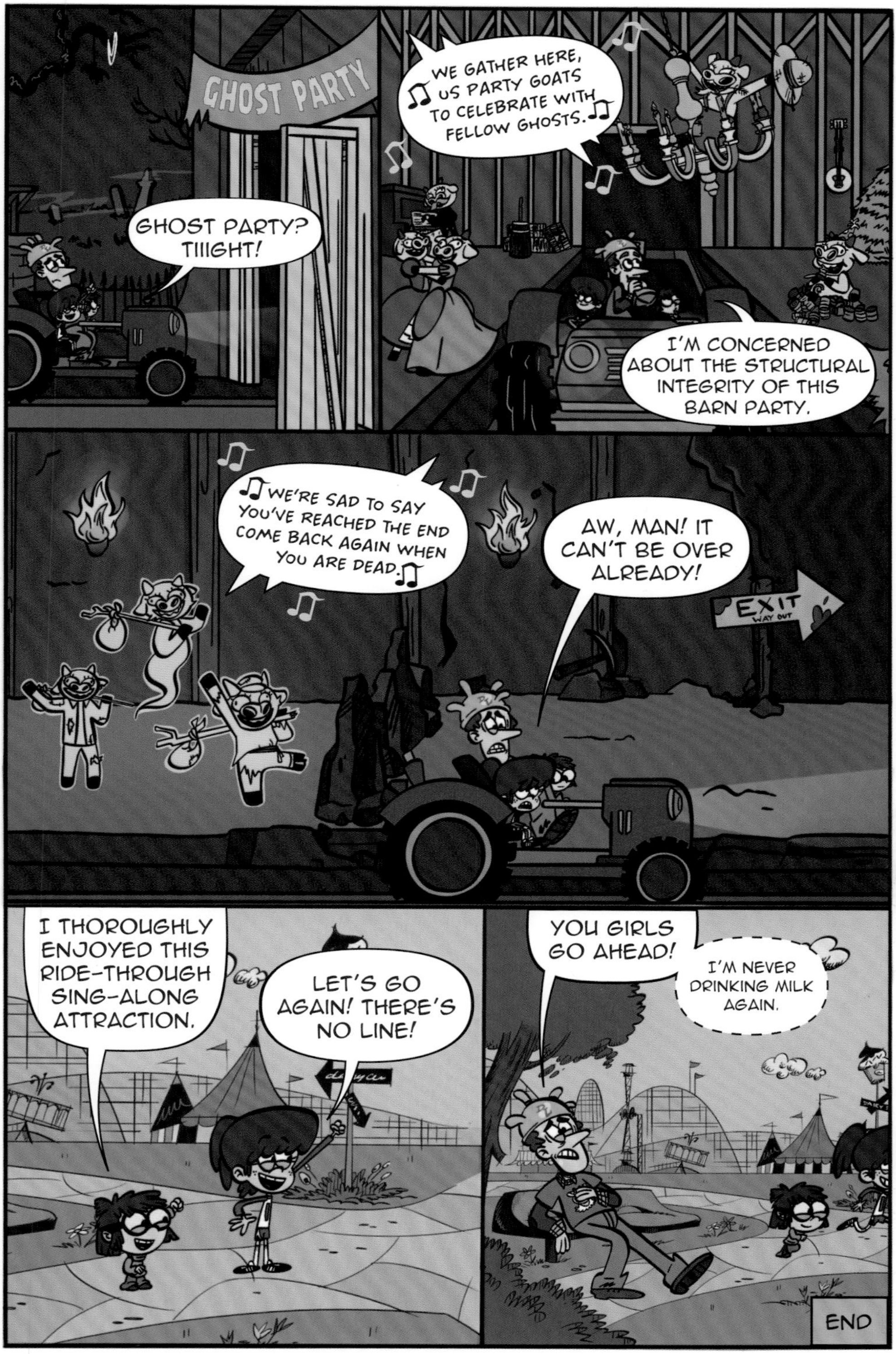
GHOST PARTY
WE GATHER HERE, US PARTY GOATS TO CELEBRATE WITH FELLOW GHOSTS.
GHOST PARTY? TIIIGHT!
I'M CONCERNED ABOUT THE STRUCTURAL INTEGRITY OF THIS BARN PARTY.
WE'RE SAD TO SAY YOU'VE REACHED THE END COME BACK AGAIN WHEN YOU ARE DEAD.
AW, MAN! IT CAN'T BE OVER ALREADY!
EXIT WAY OUT
I THOROUGHLY ENJOYED THIS RIDE-THROUGH SING-ALONG ATTRACTION.
LET'S GO AGAIN! THERE'S NO LINE!
YOU GIRLS GO AHEAD!
I'M NEVER DRINKING MILK AGAIN.
END

"LUCKY STREAK"

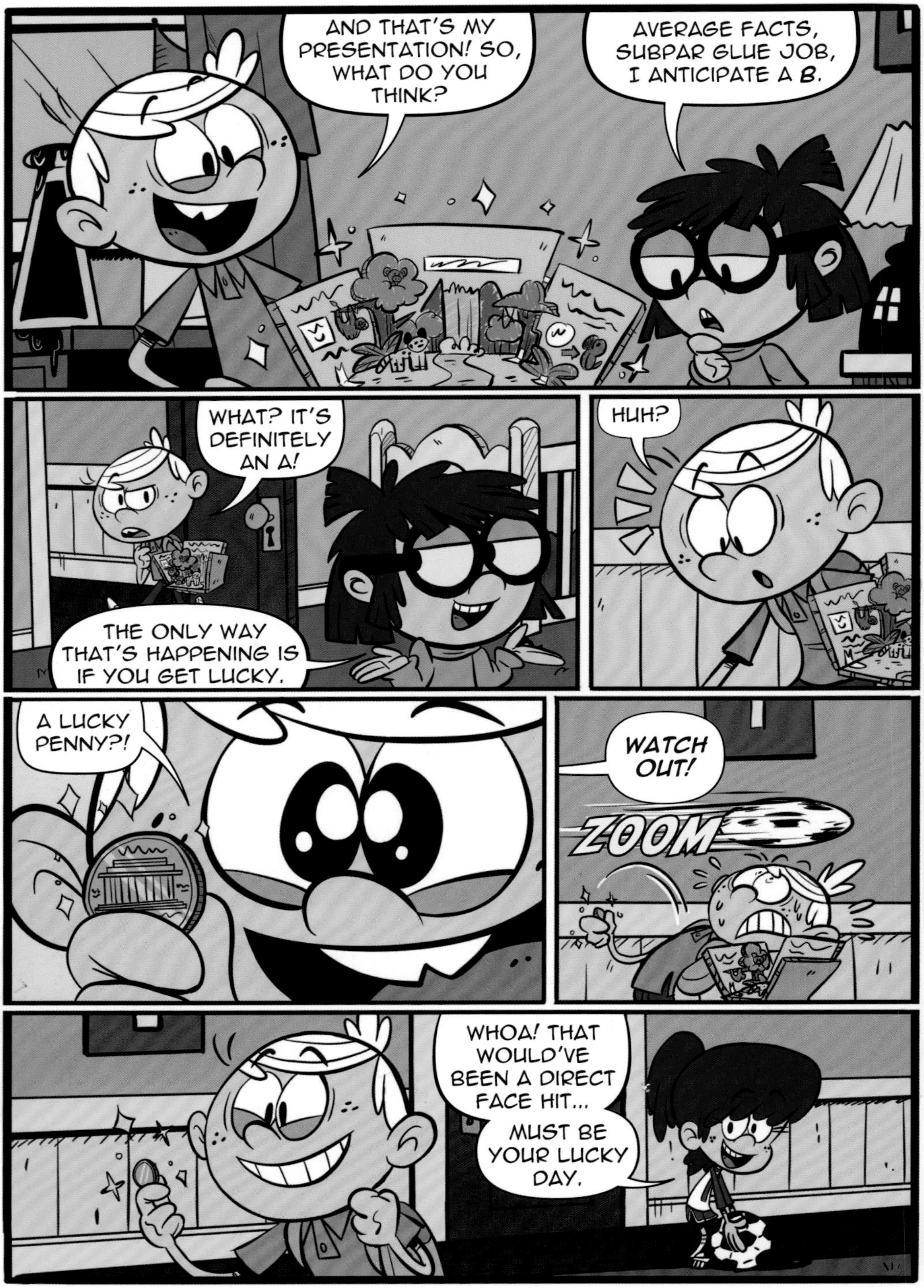
AND THAT'S MY PRESENTATION! SO, WHAT DO YOU THINK?
AVERAGE FACTS, SUBPAR GLUE JOB, I ANTICIPATE A B.
WHAT? IT'S DEFINITELY AN A!
THE ONLY WAY THAT'S HAPPENING IS IF YOU GET LUCKY.
HUH?
A LUCKY PENNY?!
WATCH OUT!
ZOOM
WHOA! THAT WOULD'VE BEEN A DIRECT FACE HIT...
MUST BE YOUR LUCKY DAY.

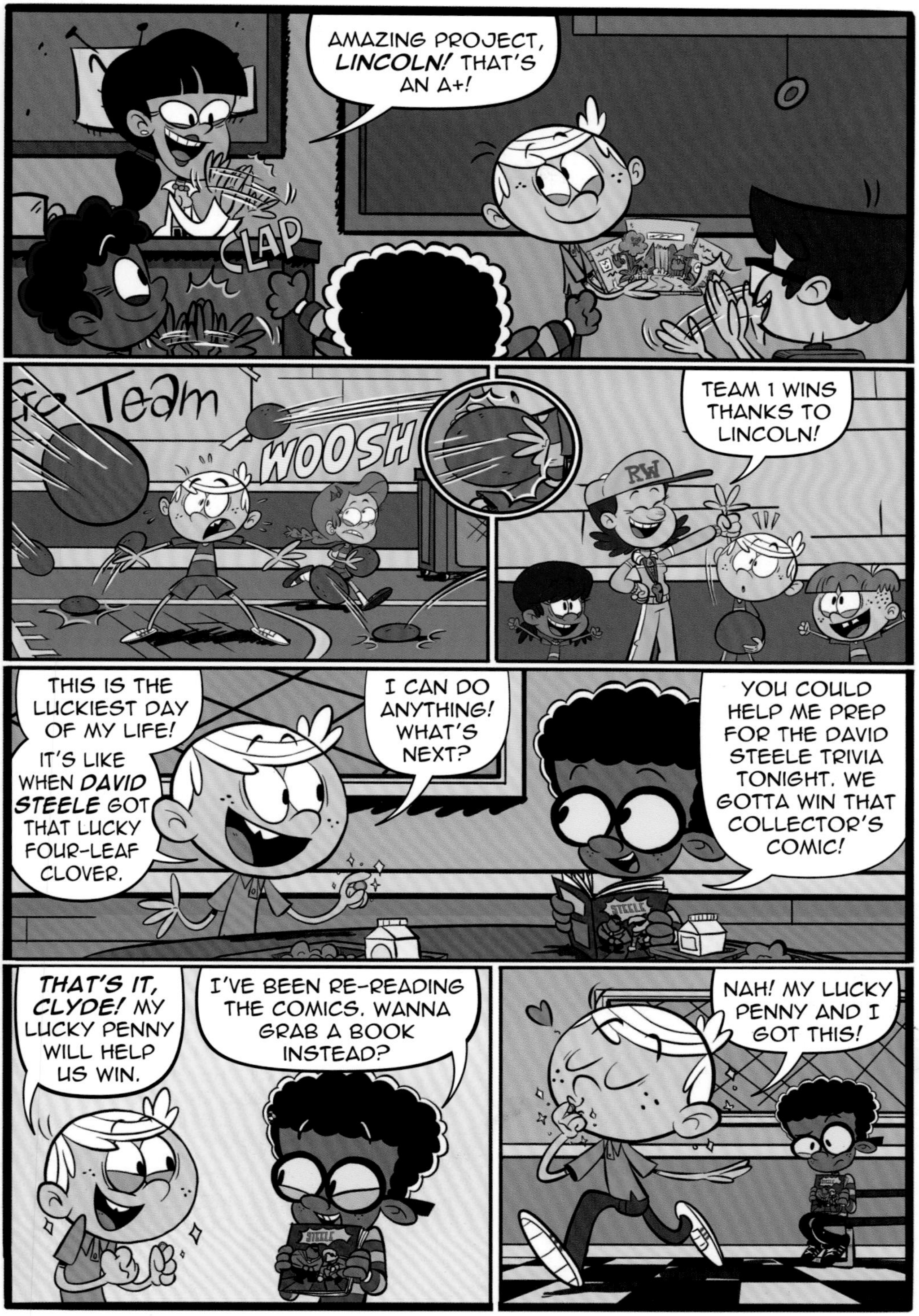
AMAZING PROJECT, LINCOLN! THAT'S AN A+!
CLAP
Go Team
WOOSH
TEAM 1 WINS THANKS TO LINCOLN!
RW
THIS IS THE LUCKIEST DAY OF MY LIFE!
IT'S LIKE WHEN DAVID STEELE GOT THAT LUCKY FOUR-LEAF CLOVER.
I CAN DO ANYTHING! WHAT'S NEXT?
YOU COULD HELP ME PREP FOR THE DAVID STEELE TRIVIA TONIGHT. WE GOTTA WIN THAT COLLECTOR'S COMIC!
STEELE
THAT'S IT, CLYDE! MY LUCKY PENNY WILL HELP US WIN.
I'VE BEEN RE-READING THE COMICS. WANNA GRAB A BOOK INSTEAD?
STEELE
NAH! MY LUCKY PENNY AND I GOT THIS!

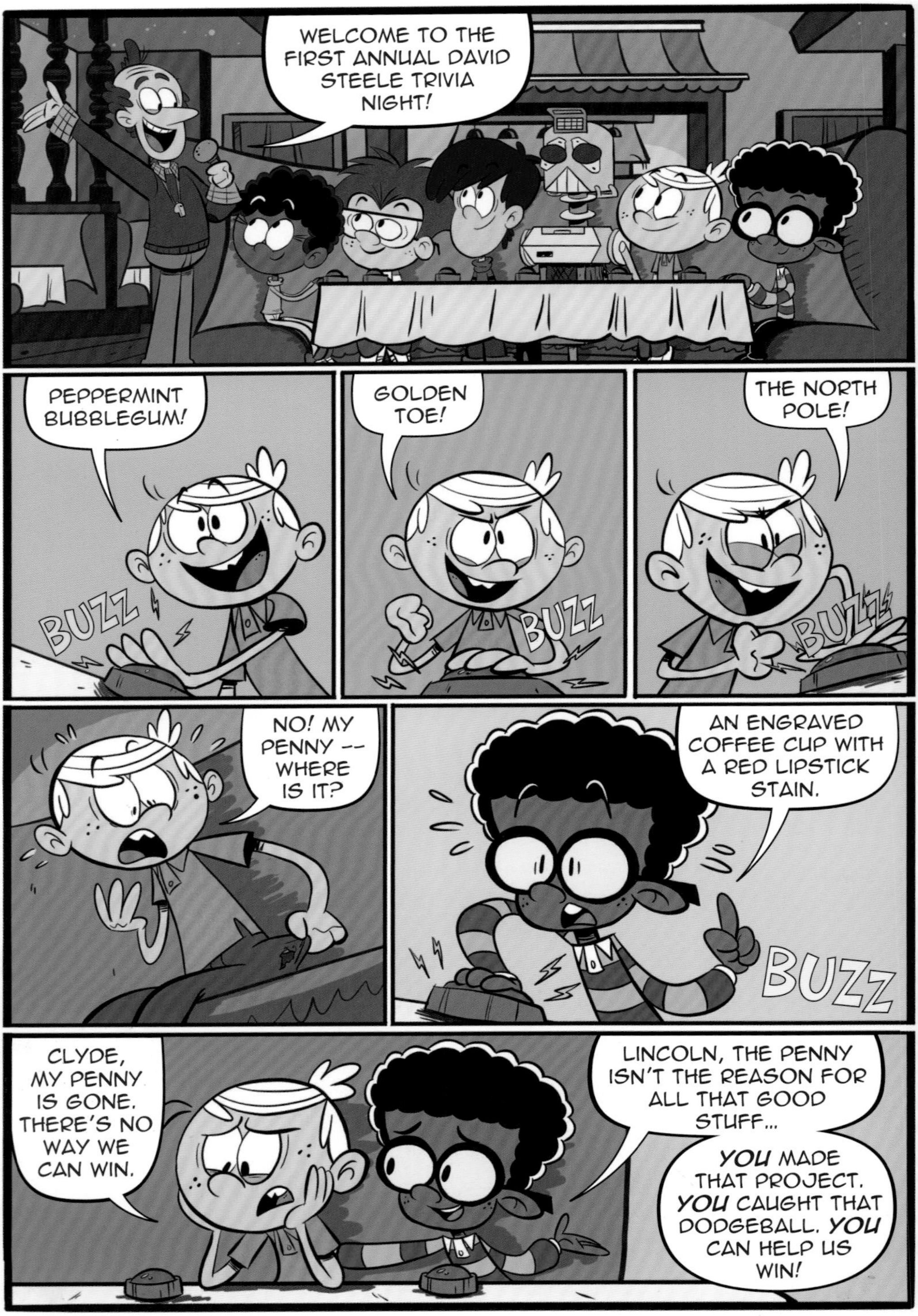
WELCOME TO THE FIRST ANNUAL DAVID STEELE TRIVIA NIGHT!
PEPPERMINT BUBBLEGUM!
BUZZ
GOLDEN TOE!
BUZZ
THE NORTH POLE!
BUZZ
NO! MY PENNY -- WHERE IS IT?
AN ENGRAVED COFFEE CUP WITH A RED LIPSTICK STAIN.
BUZZ
CLYDE, MY PENNY IS GONE. THERE'S NO WAY WE CAN WIN.
LINCOLN, THE PENNY ISN'T THE REASON FOR ALL THAT GOOD STUFF...
YOU MADE THAT PROJECT. YOU CAUGHT THAT DODGEBALL. YOU CAN HELP US WIN!

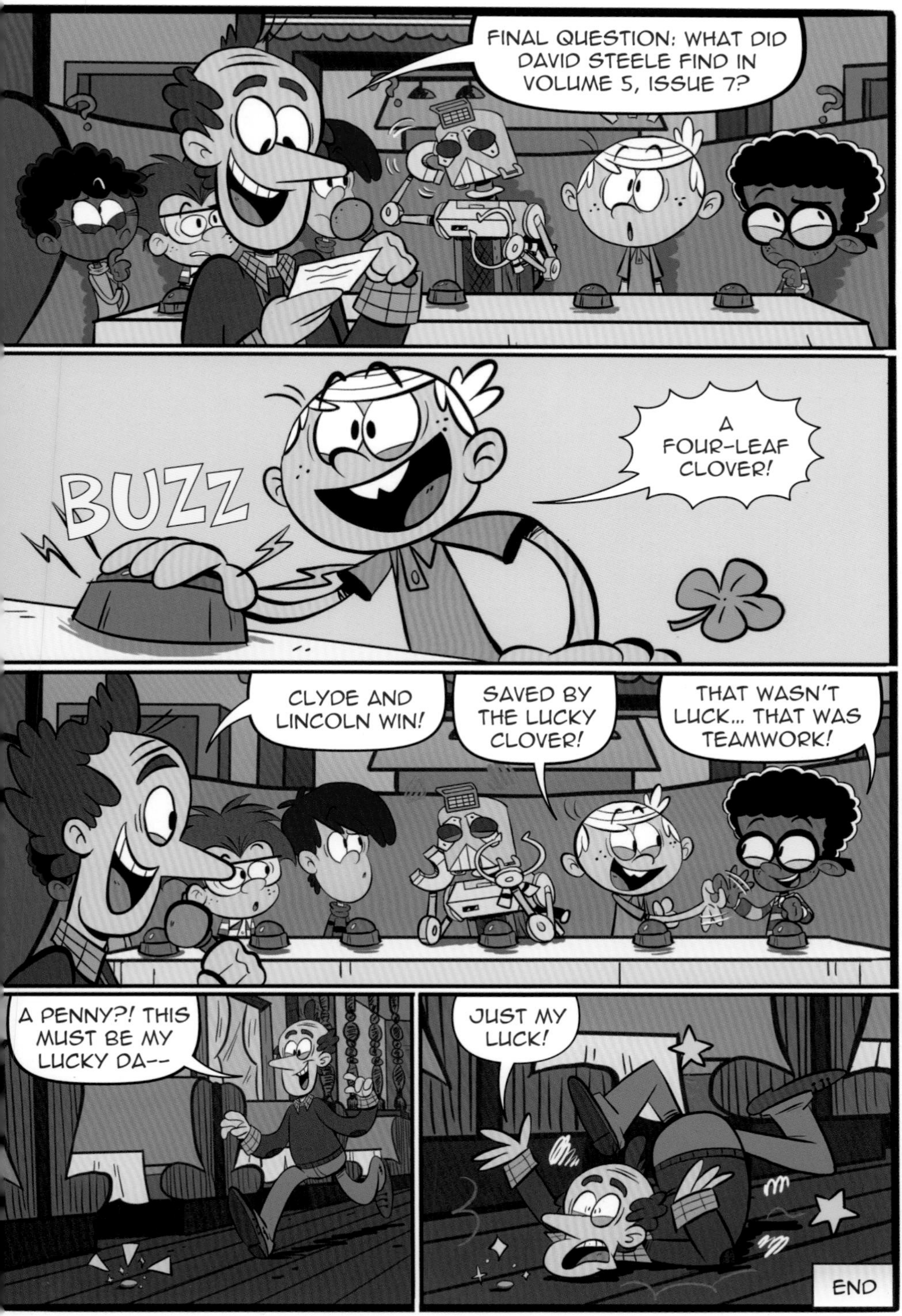

FINAL QUESTION: WHAT DID DAVID STEELE FIND IN VOLUME 5, ISSUE 7?
BUZZ
A FOUR-LEAF CLOVER!
CLYDE AND LINCOLN WIN!
SAVED BY THE LUCKY CLOVER!
THAT WASN'T LUCK... THAT WAS TEAMWORK!
A PENNY?! THIS MUST BE MY LUCKY DA--
JUST MY LUCK!
END

COMING SOON!

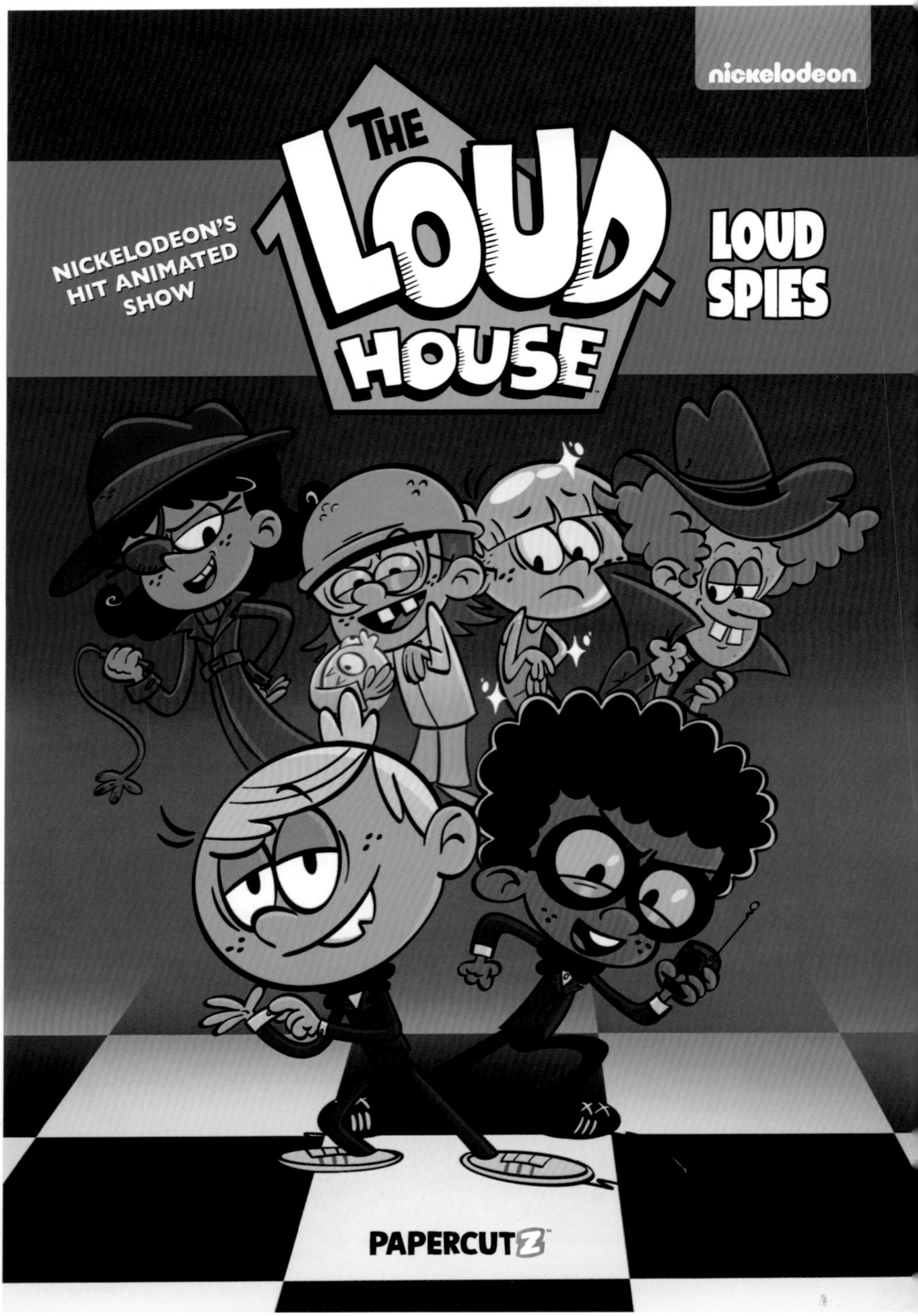

nickelodeon
NICKELODEON'S HIT ANIMATED SHOW
THE LOUD HOUSE
LOUD SPIES
PAPERCUTZ

Sneak a peek at THE LOUD HOUSE SPY SPECIAL!

"BUBBLE TROUBLE"

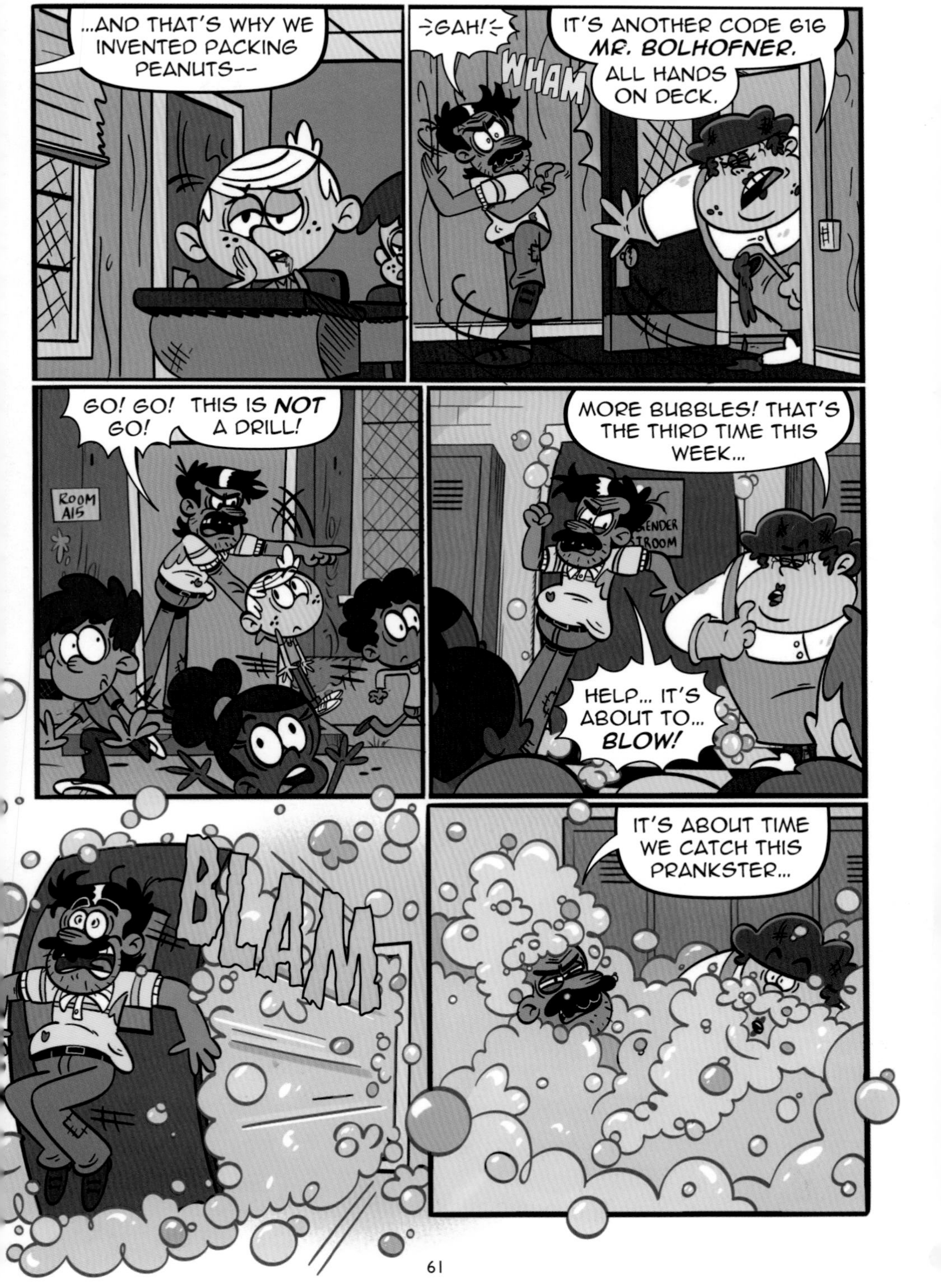
...AND THAT'S WHY WE INVENTED PACKING PEANUTS--
GAH!
WHAM
IT'S ANOTHER CODE 616 MR. BOLHOFNER. ALL HANDS ON DECK.
GO! GO! GO!
THIS IS NOT A DRILL!
ROOM A15
MORE BUBBLES! THAT'S THE THIRD TIME THIS WEEK...
HELP... IT'S ABOUT TO... BLOW!
BLAM
IT'S ABOUT TIME WE CATCH THIS PRANKSTER...

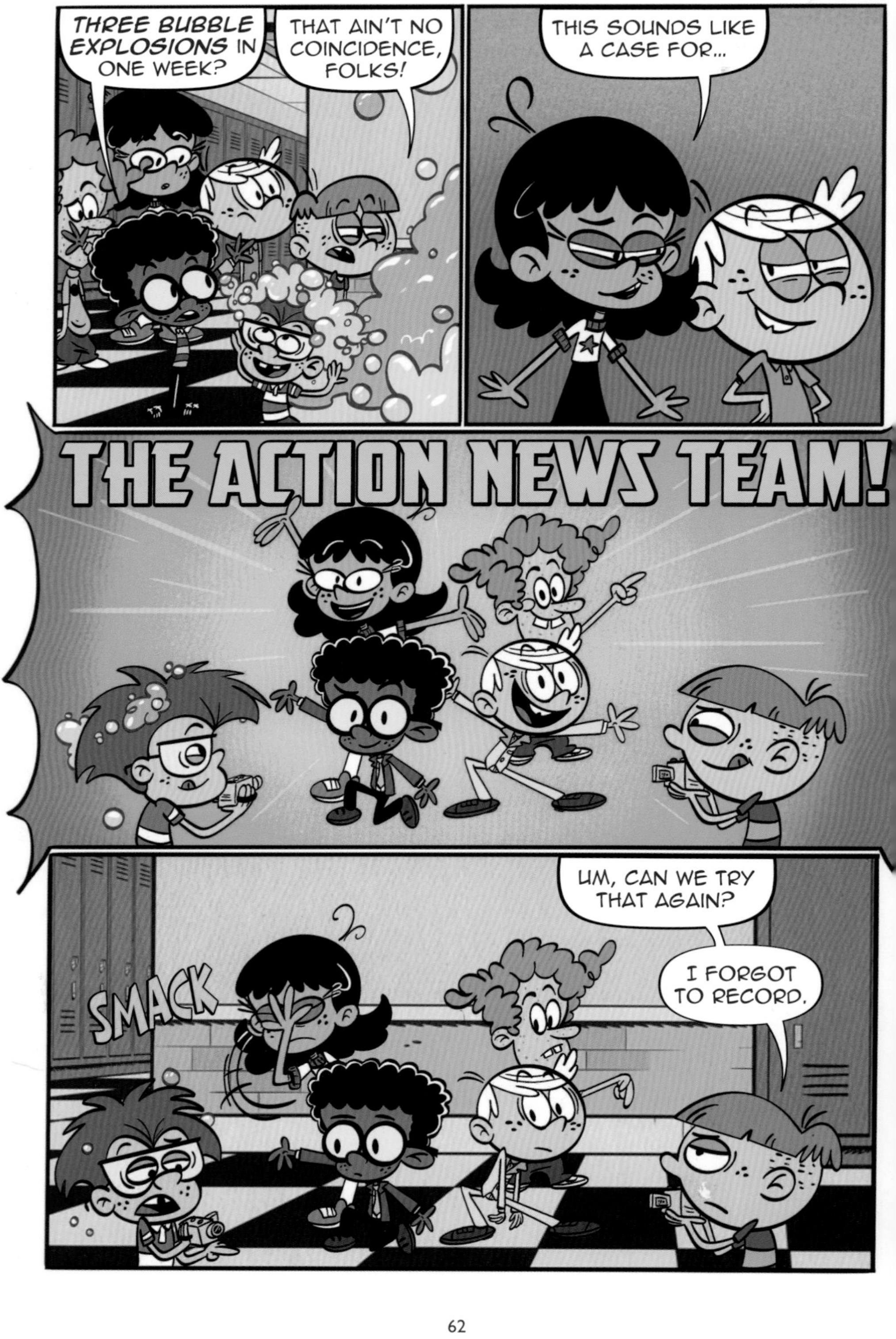
THREE BUBBLE EXPLOSIONS IN ONE WEEK?
THAT AIN'T NO COINCIDENCE, FOLKS!
THIS SOUNDS LIKE A CASE FOR...
THE ACTION NEWS TEAM!
UM, CAN WE TRY THAT AGAIN?
I FORGOT TO RECORD.
SMACK

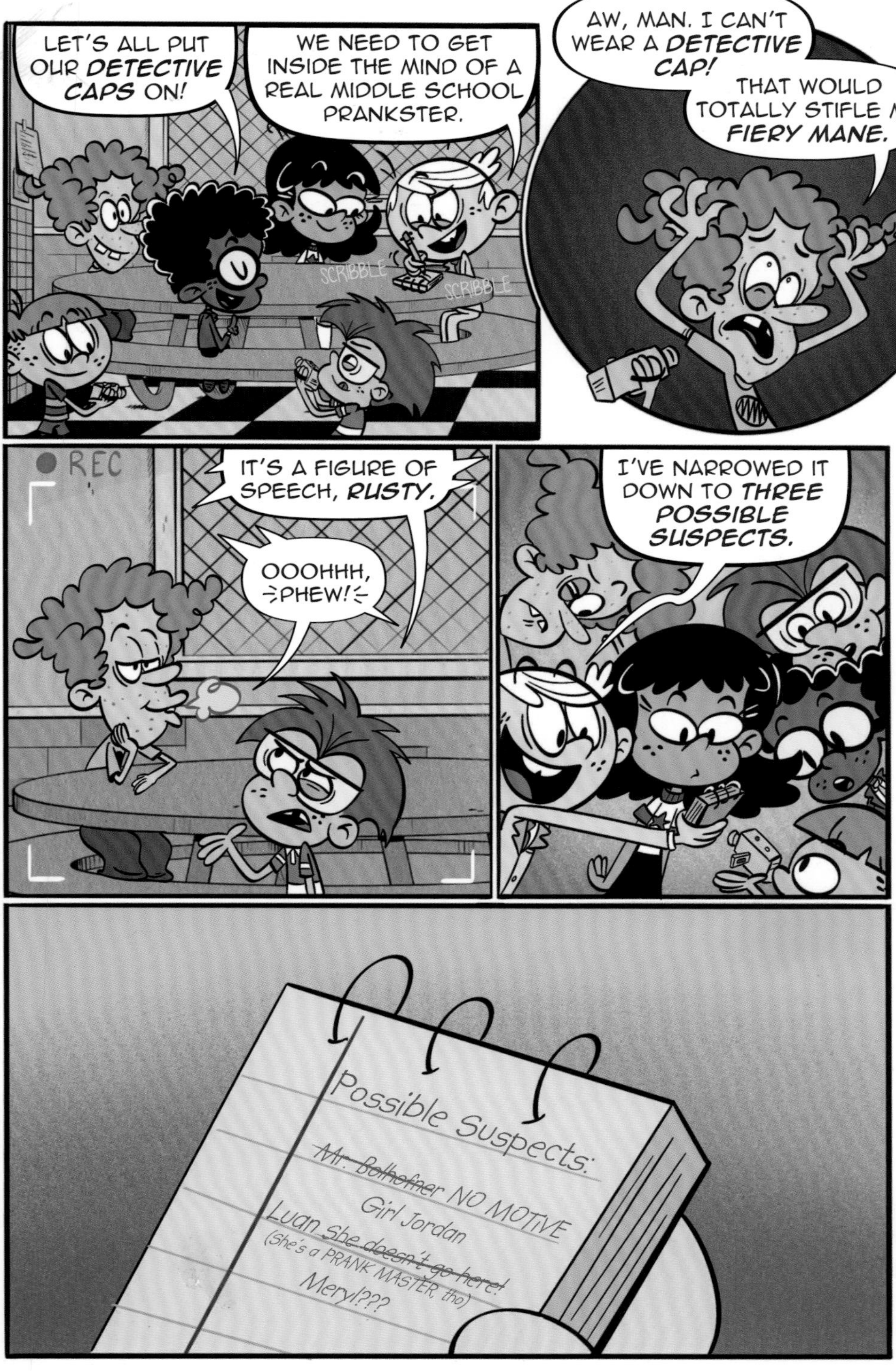
LET'S ALL PUT OUR DETECTIVE CAPS ON!
WE NEED TO GET INSIDE THE MIND OF A REAL MIDDLE SCHOOL PRANKSTER.
SCRIBBLE
SCRIBBLE
AW, MAN. I CAN'T WEAR A DETECTIVE CAP!
THAT WOULD TOTALLY STIFLE MY FIERY MANE.
REC
IT'S A FIGURE OF SPEECH, RUSTY.
OOOHHH, PHEW!
I'VE NARROWED IT DOWN TO THREE POSSIBLE SUSPECTS.
Possible Suspects:
~~Mr. Bolhofner~~ NO MOTIVE
Girl Jordan
Luan ~~She doesn't go here!~~
(She's a PRANK MASTER, tho)
Meryl!???

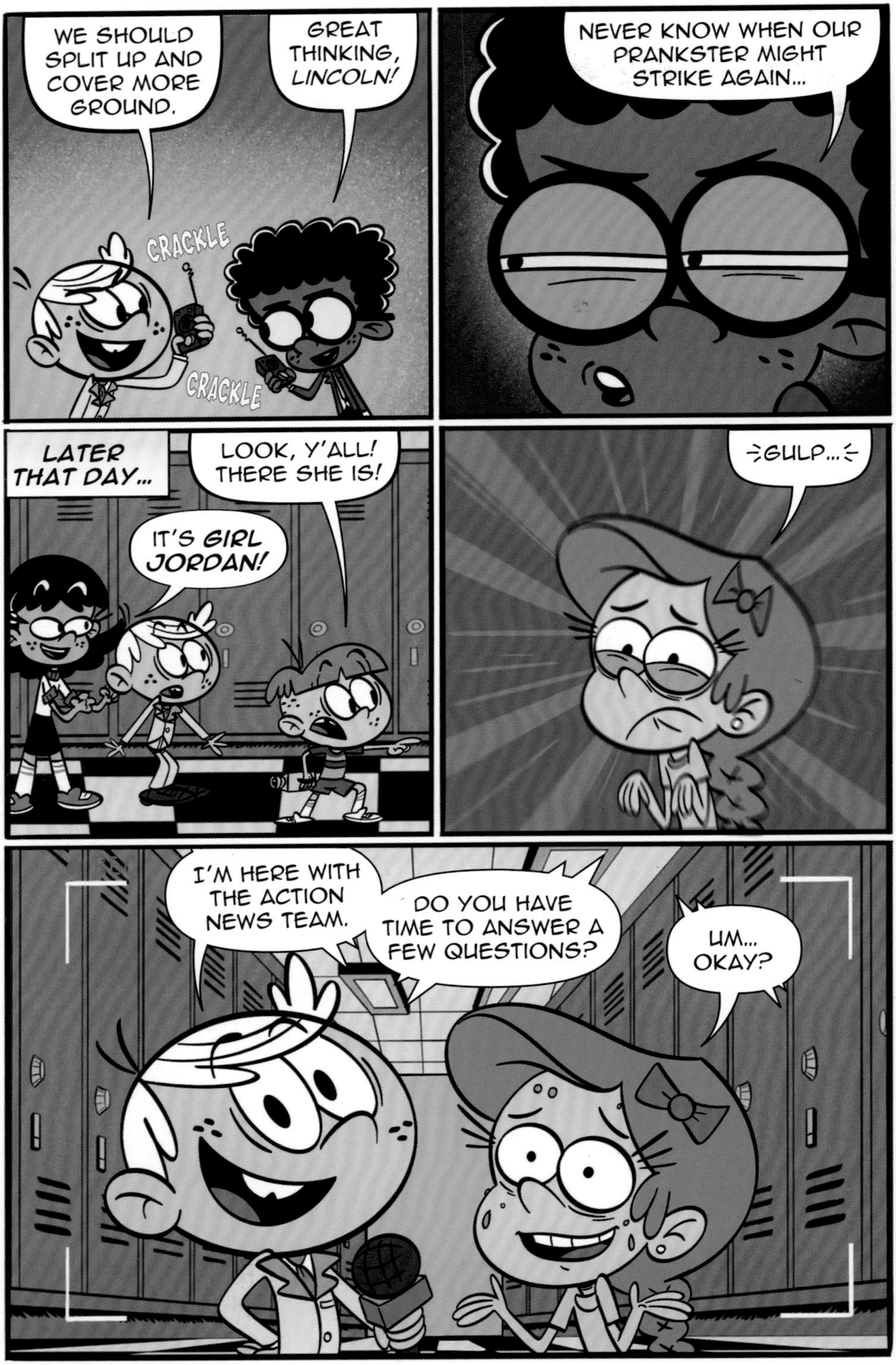
WE SHOULD SPLIT UP AND COVER MORE GROUND.
GREAT THINKING, LINCOLN!
CRACKLE
CRACKLE
NEVER KNOW WHEN OUR PRANKSTER MIGHT STRIKE AGAIN...
LATER THAT DAY...
LOOK, Y'ALL! THERE SHE IS!
IT'S GIRL JORDAN!
GULP...
I'M HERE WITH THE ACTION NEWS TEAM.
DO YOU HAVE TIME TO ANSWER A FEW QUESTIONS?
UM... OKAY?

Find out who done it in the LOUD HOUSE SPY SPECIAL - available wherever fine books are found!

GET A MOOVE ON AT DAIRY

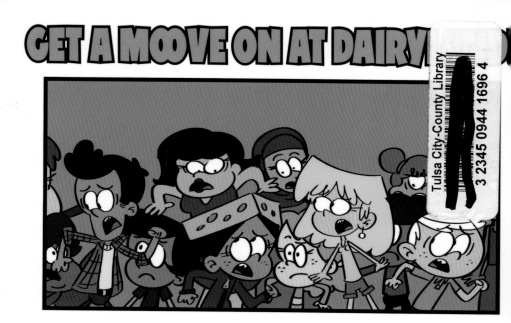

Lincoln Loud is the man with a plan, but can his plans for Dairyland Amoosement Park withstand the force of his sisters? When he loses nose-goes, Lincoln's on Lily duty – and Lily's not tall enough for the fun rides! Can Lily grow up in time to ride Fly Me to the Moo? And what happens when the Seas O' Cheese ride breaks down? Plus, Ronnie Anne swings by, and Bobby, Lori, Ronnie Anne and Lincoln take the PERFECT picture. But where did Bobby put it? The hunt is on – will Tippy the Cow help?

AND: There's a new star in the Royal Woods High Theater Department! But can Luan and her pals share the spotlight?

PLUS: Another case for the Action News Team!

Featuring all-new stories from the talented creators of the Emmy Award winning show THE LOUD HOUSE and THE CASAGRANDES!

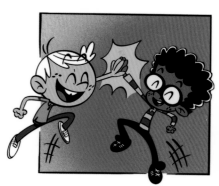

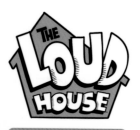

THE LOUD HOUSE

nickelodeon

papercutz.co

PAPERCUTZ
DISCOVER IMAGINATIVE NEW WORLDS

T#988425
$7.99 US / $10.99 CAN
ISBN: 978-1-5458-1056-9
nickelodeon.tv

9 781545 810569 507

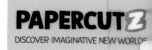